WHAT FLOWERS REMEMBER

To Cindy —
memories are the
story of life!

what flowers remember

Shannon Wiersbitzky

♡
Shannon Wiersbitzky

namelos
South Hampton, New Hampshire

Library of Congress Control Number: 2013932380

ISBN 978-1-60898-166-3 (hardcover : alk. paper)
ISBN 978-1-60898-167-0 (paperback : alk. paper)
ISBN 978-1-60898-168-7 (ebook)

www.namelos.com

For Grandpa, who never forgot my voice

April

"Tell me your first memory," said Mae. "I mean your very first one."

The creek was running high that spring. Me and my best friend Mae were lying on the hill above the water, our faces turned toward the warmth. I felt like a morning glory.

I sat up, blinking at the light. The long grass tickled. I picked a green blade and peeled back pieces while I talked.

"Colors," I said. "It was the Fourth of July. I was maybe three or four."

Mae shook her head. "No one remembers that far back, Delia."

"Well, *I* do."

I crossed my arms tight against my chest and gave her one of those looks that said I wasn't going to argue about it. I knew Mae was just plain wrong, because that day stuck in my head and I won't forget it even after I'm dead. In fact, when Mae and I meet at the pearly gates, I'm going to welcome her in and then, just to make her mad, I'm going to tell her about that day all over again.

I remembered a blue blanket, a picnic with Mama. Against the emerald-green grass on Butler Hill, which was just behind the high school, that blanket made me think about swimming. I jumped and played and pretended to splash until I ended up headfirst in the deviled eggs. Mama gave me a scolding. After that I sat real still.

"There were fireworks," I said.

Tucker's Ferry, West Virginia, may be a small town, but we have big celebrations. There isn't a holiday that goes by without some sort of parade, flag raising, wreath laying, or explosion. That Fourth of July was my favorite. It was the kind of night where fireflies danced and mosquitoes buzzed in and out, tasting everyone in the crowd.

"Describe them," said Mae. Even though she doubted my remembering, she still wanted to hear the story. She closed her eyes, waiting for me to paint her a picture with my words.

"First there was a thin line of color that shot straight up through the night sky. It was blood red, the color of Old Red's roses. Know the ones I mean? The ones that grow along the edge of the fence in the back?"

I glanced at Mae. She nodded.

"Then when that line had all but disappeared against the velvety dark, it exploded into a big flowery ball. For a moment it stayed there, hanging perfectly still in the sky, and then it wilted, those petals falling one by one to the ground." I held my arms out wide, lifting my face to the clouds. "I remember holding my hands out like this, hoping I could catch a little bit of that color."

Mae sighed. "I wish July Fourth wasn't so far away. I'd like some fireworks right now."

The snap of a branch underfoot caught our attention. There, coming down the path, was Tommy Parker. If he couldn't find us anywhere else, chances were good he'd find us at the creek.

Tommy was almost as tall as the ladies who gathered at the post office to talk to Miss Martha, but they still pinched his cheeks and told him how cute he was. There's no accounting for the opinions of old ladies. They think everyone is cute.

"He's sweet on you," whispered Mae.

Our first year of middle school had done nothing to improve Mae's poor whispering skills. I held a finger to my lips. I was almost thankful that Tommy was coming, because otherwise she'd have been all over me, getting all doe-eyed, telling me what she'd heard from other kids at school and then quizzing me about my feelings. There were no feelings. End of subject.

"Hey, Tommy," I said.

"We're talking about memories," Mae told him.

"What about them?" asked Tommy.

"Our first ones," I said. "Come on, tell us yours."

Well, a flush started at Tommy's neck and inched up his face like a red plague. I thought maybe he was having some sort of attack. Or that he'd somehow come down with the fastest and worst case of poison ivy in history.

"Ooh," said Mae, stretching the word out like carnival taffy. "It must be embarrassing."

I grinned. "I bet you were bad and got spanked. Probably deserved it too."

Tommy shook his head.

"Let me think," said Mae. "You ran naked through church when you were a baby." She tilted her head. "I think *I* might remember that, actually."

His face went back to normal color. "I'm not telling," he said. "It's none of your business what my first memory was."

I rolled my eyes. Like Tommy Parker's first memory was so super special. That boy drove me mad. He made everything harder.

3

The creek was still too cold for swimming, but every now and then we'd wander to the edge and dip our toes in, sliding them over the rocks at the bottom. We did that all afternoon. Then the sun began to fade and we headed back down the path.

When I got home, Mama was in the kitchen doing dishes. Sometimes we'd let them pile up in the sink until the pile started tipping over, and then we'd wash. I pulled a dishtowel from a hook on the wall and stood next to her. As she set each clean, wet dish on the counter, I dried it and put it away.

"What's your first memory, Mama?" I asked, adding a bowl to the cupboard.

Mama didn't say a thing, just kept washing. A soap bubble slid down her wrist and onto her arm. Then I saw her glance at the ceiling, and I knew she was thinking.

"Come on," I said. "Tell me." Mama wasn't usually one for sharing. But I had a feeling this story would come out.

"I was maybe three or four," she started.

I couldn't help but grin even though Mae wasn't there. It was one of those smiles where the corners of your mouth go way up but none of your teeth show.

"I had a shiny new tricycle that I wanted to ride to my grandparents' house. They lived just down the block at the time." Mama stared off into that far-away place that people go to when they're pulling up old thoughts. "It was summer, and the dandelions had popped up like yellow mushrooms all over our yard. I picked a whole handful to bring to Grandma. My tricycle even had a small basket on the front. In went my bouquet and off I pedaled."

"What happened then?" I asked.

Mama's eyes snapped back to the dishes. "Well, I got to Grandma's and all those dandelions were about as perky as a lump of cottage cheese. I cried and cried."

I could picture those yellow heads hanging low, the pale green stems limp. There is nothing in the world more pathetic than a bunch of wilted dandelions.

"Grandma got those weeds in water and Grandpa made toast for me. He covered it with butter and honey. My grandparents thought honey was a cure for most anything. They'd smear it on cuts like salve and pour out spoonfuls at even the hint of stomach ache."

The sun shone in through the kitchen window, making Mama's blond hair shimmer.

"Did it work?" I asked.

Mama paused with a dish in her hand. "That honey was as sweet as summer. By the time I finished the toast, my tears were dry and those dandelions had perked up too." She started washing again. "So, yes, I guess it did."

"I never heard that story before," I said.

Mama didn't say anything else.

I didn't mind, though. I kept taking wet dishes, drying them, and then putting them away. While I dried, I thought about Mama's story. It's funny how even when you've lived with someone your whole life, they can still surprise you.

That night I lay in bed with the window partway open. I listened to the chant of the toads, the chirp of the crickets, and from the wood, the sharp call of the whippoorwill.

One of the Thread-Bears, the sewing ladies at church, told me that the whippoorwill can sense when a person is dying.

"They know the exact moment when a soul leaves its body," she said as she pushed the needle through her fabric and back up the other side. "If they're close by, they can catch it as it goes."

Even though the weather was warm, I pulled the sheet close, tucking it under my chin. All curled up, I stared into the darkness and listened to those birds. I thought about the souls that might be floating through the air right that very moment.

I didn't ask the sewing ladies what the whippoorwills did with a soul after they caught one. Maybe those birds brought it home and tucked it in their nest, weaving it in and through all the other twigs. I bet souls are better than down feathers. The good ones, anyway. They probably make that nest feel softer than cotton. Or maybe, when the whippoorwills are flying around in the night, they carry those souls high into the clouds and let them go.

May

Most folks probably think gardens only get tended when they're blooming. But most folks would be wrong. According to the almanac, a proper gardener does something every single month. Old Red Clancy was definitely a proper gardener. That's why I enrolled myself in the Clancy School of Gardening. If I was going to learn about flowers, I wanted to learn from the best.

Old Red got in the habit of meeting me at the bus when the weather was warm, and together we'd walk the few blocks to his house. Our lessons began as soon as we arrived at the garden. At first he started slow, teaching me which plants were weeds and which were color in waiting. I tried to hurry him along during that part, but after I murdered a whole bed of black-eyed Susans, we went back to the basics.

Eventually we moved on to feeding. I had no idea that flowers needed to eat. Old Red's particularly liked coffee and eggs.

"Coffee grounds keep the slugs away," said Old Red. "Nasty creatures. You get one feasting and pretty soon there's an army."

"What are the eggshells for?" I asked.

"Now, Miss Delia," said Old Red, "those are for the roses."

Besides being able to mix up the right food for an entire garden, I bet I can recite the names of over a hundred flowers now. And some of them in Latin. I'm not sure why that's important, because I don't know a single person in Tucker's Ferry who speaks Latin. Old Red insisted, though—said it was the way he'd been taught. I liked that, even though I fussed about it for weeks.

Sometimes I used those Latin names on Mae, just to annoy her.

"We cut a bunch of *Delphinium exaltatum* yesterday," I said. "They were bluer than the sky."

Mae rolled her eyes, one hand on her hip. "You know I haven't the foggiest notion of what you're talking about."

Every time I did that it drove Mae a little crazy. I feature I did it about once a week.

During the thick of the summer, Old Red taught me how to tend the blossoms, pulling off the dead blooms and dropping them into a bucket. Other flowers I cut, leaving long stems so we could put them in water. There was a row of Mason jars lining the window in his kitchen.

At first it didn't seem right to cut all those flowers. They were so beautiful right there in the garden. The only thing my complaining got me was another gardening lesson.

"Now don't go getting sentimental on me," said Old Red. "Cutting is the best way to keep them healthy. You watch. There's one pretty flower here now, but in another week or two there will be three in its place. When tended the right way, beauty multiplies."

Mama bought me my own pair of pruning shears. The grip was soft in all the right spots, the blade sharp as a razor. On and on through the garden we went, Old Red keeping up a constant chatter. With all the information he had in there, it's a wonder his head didn't explode. I took it in. Then, when he sat on the porch for a rest, I'd talk to the flowers.

I kept my voice quiet, a whisper, barely loud enough for them to hear. Talking to them felt right. Like they were friends.

"Old Red and I haven't always been close," I said. "Before last summer I was a little afraid of him." I gave Rex an eyeball as he shuffled near the fence, sniffing. "And I was definitely afraid of that mangy old mutt. I swear that dog almost ate me a few times."

The flowers nodded in the breeze, encouraging me to go on. Petals of a flower stroked my hand. They felt silky soft.

"But Mr. Clancy isn't mean at all. You probably know that already."

I picked up my bucket and went on to the next bed of flowers. They were leaning forward, waiting for me to continue.

"In fact, besides Mae and Tommy, he was the first person to help me last summer when the house needed fixing." I shook my head, still barely able to believe it.

Those flowers and I talked about everything. Most afternoons it wasn't anything serious. Over time I could almost hear those flowers talking back, telling me which blooms to cut and which to save.

There wasn't a single person in town who didn't admire Old Red Clancy's garden. People drove by his house once the blooming began, simply to stare at the color. I'd be sitting on his porch and there they'd come, moving so slow I could have delivered glasses of lemonade if I'd taken the notion.

Once when I was giving Rex a scratch behind the ear, I watched a woman drive by and park on the other side of the street. When she climbed out, it was almost as if she'd come from church—which couldn't have been the case, seeing as it was a Tuesday, and all of the evening services in Tucker's Ferry were on Wednesday night.

When she got to the fence, her eyes gobbled up the flowers like they were the five-dollar buffet special. She ran her hand along the blooms. When she set down her purse and opened it up, I knew exactly what she was planning. Seeing as I'd stolen Old Red's flowers before myself, let's just say that I recognized a crook when I saw one. I was sure she was going for the Sleeping Beauty rose. That one was white as fresh snow and the envy of every lady gardener in all of Tucker's Ferry. Instead she reached for the brownest, deadest, driest-looking stem. That's when I realized what she was after. Seeds.

I gave a little cough, then a louder one, and asked in my most ice-cream-sundae voice if I could help her with anything. That woman hightailed it back to her car so fast she almost lost a shoe. While I was laughing, I came up with an idea.

Ideas are funny that way, popping up when they're least expected. As that idea was churning in my head, my left eye began to twitch. That's when I got really excited. My eye only did that with the good ideas.

Old Red and I could start a business. A business selling flower seeds.

Old Red had what they call heirloom flowers. In fact, his garden was bursting with years of history. Heirloom flowers are born from seeds that have never been doctored by a factory. They're the kind of seeds that have been handed down from generation to generation. These flowers had been growing here in Tucker's Ferry for hundreds of years. They grew in the gardens of his great-grandparents' great-grandparents, and when the flowers died, they collected the seeds, marking and saving them for the following year. Then, when they had children, they divided those seeds and handed them down. According to Old Red, flowers like that are not easy to find anymore.

While gathering seeds in my hand, some big, some as tiny as a grain of sand, I've wondered if they hold any memory of the flowers before them. What they saw, what they heard, how to survive in times of drought, or anything at all about the people who tended them. If they do, I wonder what the next seeds will remember about me and Old Red.

June

The last day of school was just about the best day ever. The teachers were itching to leave, the kids were bouncing off the walls, even the principal walked around watching the clock, waiting for the bell that marked the official beginning of summer. The best part of the last day was talking about summer plans. I told everyone about the seed business I was starting with Old Red. I'd combined initials from our last names, Burns and Clancy, and called it B & C Gardening. It sounded old-fashioned, and when I said it aloud, it rang in my ears.

There were lots of folks who needed my help. The Buckle family had a yard that looked sadder than a bare patch of concrete. Then there was the Wiley place, down the road from the IGA, which was our local grocery store. The Wileys never planted a thing, and mowed only when the weeds reached the windows. That place looked worse than the abandoned farmhouse down on Pennypacker Road—and that's being nice about it. I figured with a few flyers and some door-to-door sales we'd be raking in the money in no time.

When Tommy and I climbed off the bus, Old Red was there as usual, waiting.

"Hey, Mr. Clancy," said Tommy.

"Well, good afternoon, young Mr. Parker," said Old Red. "And hello to you, Ms. Burns." He gave me a little bow.

Old Red had a way of making me feel like a lady, which is saying something, since I was a checkerboard of cuts, scrapes, and at least one bruise at any given time. I stood taller, pushing against my backpack. I think it weighed two hundred pounds, since I had every last book and notebook and all the school supplies I'd ever owned in there.

"I thought I might tell you a story as we walk home," said Old Red.

"Are you sure these stories are true?" I cocked my head to the right and gave him a sideways glance.

"I may exaggerate," he said, "but I never lie. Clancy boys do not lie." He raised an eyebrow at Tommy. "My mother used to say that to me every day."

"Well, if they're all true, it's a wonder you're still alive," I said, sounding like Miss Martha.

"My mother used to say *that* every day, too." Old Red's cheeks were pink, his eyes bright as a shiny penny at the bottom of the creek. "Did I ever tell you the story of me and Mr. Bailey?"

Tommy shook his head. He usually ran on ahead, leaving me and Old Red in the dust, but the offer of a story was near impossible to resist. Not much different from fresh doughnuts. We moved slowly. The gravel road wasn't a good match for Mr. Clancy's bad hip and cane.

"Mr. Bailey was the bus driver in Tucker's Ferry when I was a kid. Oh, he was the meanest man south of the Mason-Dixon line. Had one eye that followed you no matter how you moved. That man hated children. And out of all the kids he picked up on his route, he hated me the most."

"Why you?" I asked. "What did you do?"

Old Red stopped to wave at the widow Carson, who was sitting on her porch, hair tied back in a kerchief, fanning herself with what looked like an old church program. "I always broke the rules. Dickie McDooley was one of my best friends. My accomplice, too."

"What kind of rules are you talking about?" asked Tommy.

I made a noise halfway between a groan and a sigh. Tommy wasn't the sharpest hoe in the field. "There are lots of rules," I said, ticking them off my fingers one by one. "Sitting in your seat, no yelling, no throwing things, no mooning the cars behind the bus, and about a hundred others."

"All good ones, too," said Old Red. "But Mr. Bailey's biggest rule was being on time. Anyone not on the bus by eight o'clock sharp got left behind. Mr. Bailey and his crazy eye waited for no one."

"How would the kids get to school if they missed the bus?" I asked.

"They'd have to walk," said Old Red. "Simple as that. Well, I used to cut it close every day. Dickie would stand on those bus steps talking up a storm, so Mr. Bailey couldn't shut the door. And there I'd be, running down the hill from my house." He lifted his cane and pointed. "I'd turn sideways, suck in my ribs, and somehow make myself thin as a sheet of paper, so as not to get crushed while Mr. Bailey was closing that door."

"I bet Mr. Bailey hated that," said Tommy.

"His knuckles would tighten on that steering wheel until I thought he might break it in half," said Old Red.

That made me laugh. It was no wonder that Mr. Clancy and I got along as well as we did. As the Thread-Bears would say, we were cut from the same cloth.

"Then one day," said Old Red, "I'm not sure if Mr. Bailey's clock was fast or mine was slow, but when I started running down that hill, Mr. Bailey closed the door. Actually, I think Dickie was home sick that day. Anyway, Mr. Bailey put the pedal down and that bus moved faster than it ever had before." Old Red nudged Tommy with his cane. "He was driving like there might be a checkered flag when he got to school."

"So what'd you do?" asked Tommy.

Good storytellers are always ready for the next question. I could see the words sitting on Old Red's tongue.

My mother is going to kill me if I'm late for school. That's what I thought," said Old Red. "But I kept running. The kids in the back could see me. They were waving and cheering." He paused, then gave us a wink. "What Mr. Bailey didn't know is that I was the state champion in the mile."

I could picture Mr. Bailey, eyebrows drawn, glancing back at all those screaming kids and holding tight to that steering wheel as the bus tore through the streets of Tucker's Ferry. I could taste the dust blowing through the bus windows.

"There must have been sweat trickling down Mr. Bailey's face as you grew bigger and bigger in that side mirror," said Tommy.

"Then," said Old Red, "just as Mr. Bailey had to shift down to second gear to round the final turn to school, I leapt and grabbed hold of that mirror."

"I bet Mr. Bailey about had a heart attack," I said, almost skipping along, bouncing on the balls of my feet.

"He was swerving left and right trying to shake me off. But I wasn't going anywhere," said Old Red. "We pulled into the school parking lot with me hanging off that mirror like a flag from a flagpole. Principal Skinner was standing there watching the whole thing, eyes wider than the cake trays the ladies bring to church on potluck Sundays."

Tommy and I laughed. So did Old Red.

"Did Mr. Bailey get in trouble?" I asked.

"Some of the words that came out of Principal Skinner's mouth were not fit for the ears of children," said Old Red. "Mr. Bailey took early retirement that year."

"What about you?" Tommy asked. "Did you do the same thing with the next bus driver?"

Old Red shook his head. "Nope. The next bus driver would keep that door open all day waiting for me. Didn't mind a bit if I was a few minutes late."

I took a deep breath, still picturing Mr. Clancy dangling from that bus. I wished I could tell stories like that. My stories didn't leave people wide-eyed, waiting for my next word, or laughing until their stomachs ached. Usually I got the facts mixed up and had to start over, and half the time I'd forgotten what I wanted to say by then. Storytelling is an art, that's all I have to say, and Old Red was the best artist in Tucker's Ferry.

Even though it was early June, we'd already had a week of temperatures in the eighties. I could feel the sweat dripping down between my shoulders underneath my backpack.

Old Red stopped walking. His face was flushed.

We were two blocks from his house, three from mine and Tommy's. We'd been this way a million times before. I bet I could have walked half the streets in Tucker's Ferry blindfolded. They were as familiar as the lines on my own hand.

Old Red stood on the corner and didn't move at all. Tommy

and I stopped too, glancing left and right, trying to figure out what was the matter. I even stared up at the branches of the trees, wondering if he'd spotted some rare bird.

"What is it, Mr. Clancy?" I asked.

Tommy kneeled down to tie his shoes.

"Nothing," said Old Red, smoothing the hair over his head.

When Tommy and I turned left, Old Red turned right, as if he didn't know the way to his very own house.

I gave him a tug on the arm. "This way, silly."

July

Anyone can forget things. One time last summer, in the middle of a heat wave, Mrs. Watkins came to church with two different shoes on. Those shoes weren't even the same height. She made her way down the center aisle, program clutched in one hand and that white vinyl purse locked in the crook of her other arm, hobbling back and forth like a drunken sailor. I almost got seasick watching her. No one said a single word about those shoes, even though I'm sure there wasn't a soul in that sanctuary who didn't notice them.

Somewhere between the third hymn and the Lord's Prayer, she must have looked down at her feet, because she tore out of that church as soon as the preacher gave the last *Amen*. Didn't stay for coffee or cookies or anything.

Of course forgetting things isn't something that happens only to old ladies. It happened to me and Mama too. A few times we left a whole bottle of fabric softener at the Speedi-King Laundromat because we were rushing to get home. It could get so hot in there during the dead of August that each breath burned going down. At CJ's Diner, where Mama waitressed, people were always leaving sunglasses, reading glasses, and pocketbooks. Once Mama even found a pair of shoes under a table. As if the person wearing them had finished dessert and then vanished.

Forgetting things is normal.

In fact, if Mae hadn't come to get me, I probably would

have forgotten the entire Fourth of July celebration that year. Or at least I'd have been late. The whole weekend was chock-full of events. Down at the park, they shot off an old war cannon. There were men dressed in navy blue uniforms who reenacted it exactly the way it would have been done back then. Tucker's Ferry liked to kick off celebrations with a bang.

Usually the best part of the holiday was the fireworks, but that year someone on the celebration committee had been inspired to paint the fire hydrants. In fact there was a contest to see who could paint the best one. Everyone in town was buzzing about it. The rules were simple. All hydrants had to be painted mostly red, white, and blue. Black was not allowed, as it made it tough for the Fire Department to find them. A fire hydrant is not something you want to lose, especially in an emergency.

Mae and I were assigned the hydrant in our neighborhood, which was on the corner by the IGA. We sat down with our paints and brushes and stared at that big hunk of silver metal. With all the bits and pieces jutting out here and there, I wasn't convinced it was going to look like much of anything when we were done.

"What should we paint?" I asked.

"How about a soldier?" she said.

"Really?" I said. "With a little face up top?" I pointed to the rounded cap of metal. "That seems too hard."

"Maybe stars, then," said Mae. "We could cover the entire thing in white stars."

I snapped my fingers. "That's it!"

"What's it?" said Mae.

"We can turn this ugly metal hydrant into a flag."

Two hours later, that's exactly what we'd done. There were wide white and red stripes running up and down. We painted the top blue. Then Mae, since it had been her idea to start with, added perfect white stars.

Miss Martha said our hydrant was one of her favorites, even though it didn't get picked by the committee as the best. That honor went to a high school kid named Owen who had won every drawing contest in the entire state and even one in Kentucky. Mae about killed me when we went to see what he'd done. Somehow Owen had managed to paint a perfect Continental soldier. The hydrant had a blue coat with a red vest underneath, white pants, and a long, thin rifle. Owen had even managed to make the top of that hydrant look like a cocked blue hat. Beats me how he did that.

I was still trying to figure it out when I went to Old Red's later that week. Rex was waiting for me. A year ago, whenever he saw me coming down the street, he'd charge at the fence, drooling and barking and slobbering all over as if he was planning to have me for supper. Now he barely lifted his chin when I came through the gate. Sometimes he'd give me a low growl, which was the closest he got to a wag. If he had a full stomach, he'd tolerate a pat on the head and then roll over on his back and wait for me to rub his belly.

Rex followed me to the garage, where I was officially kicking off B & C Gardening. Since I'd already started telling folks about it, I needed to get moving on the inventory. And that meant collecting and drying seeds.

Old Red had a wide workbench in a dark, dry corner next to his truck. It smelled of oil and wood and metal. He had saws and wrenches and screwdrivers of all sizes hanging on pegboard along the wall. It reminded me of Mr. Parker's garage. I'm not sure why men need so many tools. Mama and I do just fine without them.

Before I gathered anything, I wanted to make sure the drying area was ready. Drying is one of the most important parts. Storing wet seeds over the winter is a recipe for disaster. Either they mold and rot or they try to grow, and whichever one happens means only one thing: trouble. Not a single person in Tucker's Ferry was going to buy seeds like that.

I'd been collecting newspapers for weeks, gathering them up from neighbors on the street. If I walked down a street taking newspapers on the day they were delivered, I'd be accused of stealing. If I rang the bell politely the very next day and asked for day-old papers, well, folks were happy to see me. They'd lay them in my arms with a smile and send me on my way.

I opened up those newspapers and stacked them on the concrete floor. Then, picking up several sheets at a time, I laid them across the workbench. They'd soak up any bits of moisture left in those seeds. With a hammer I tacked down the edges, tapping baby nails just deep enough to hold the paper to the ply-wood. I'd brought a black marker and in block letters I wrote the names of the flowers I planned to collect. Then I drew thick dividing lines from top to bottom to keep from mixing anything up. Word would get around town fast if we sold someone sun-flowers and then marigolds popped up instead. Gossip traveled faster than the train through Tucker's Ferry.

In the garden my hands moved quickly, deadheading the lilies that had bloomed back in June. That way all that plant's energy would go into making seeds. The ones I left would be ready in September.

I snapped the dry, brown flowers from the marigolds and brought them to the garage. One by one I gently pinched and pulled the two ends apart. There in the middle were the seeds. They were long, black, slender, and sharp on the ends, like tiny little darts. I set them across the paper.

With the gardening shears, I cut the tops from the blue bachelor buttons. I barely needed to touch them and their seeds fell right out. Next year there would be a swath of blue across Tucker's Ferry.

The seeds that were the most fun to gather were from the poppies. Old Red had some that were fiery red. Once the flowers died, only a small green pod was left. When it dried to a sandy brown, the seeds were ready. I cut a few pods, being careful to catch them in a paper bag. Back in the garage I shook that bag like I was fixing to make fried chicken with Miss Martha. I picked out the empty pods, then poured those tiny seeds onto the paper. There must have been thousands of them.

"We're off to a great start, ladies," I said to the flowers when I got back to the yard. "Keep up the good work."

"You talking to the flowers again?" Old Red gave me a shout. He was swinging on the porch, watching me sweat.

"No," I called back.

Almost directly after I answered, he asked me again. "You talking to the flowers?"

I gave him my best eye roll.

Old Red had been doing that a lot lately. Repeating things over and over as if I hadn't heard him well enough the first time. I chalked it up to the heat.

I put my head down and whispered more quietly.

When Tommy showed up and walked straight to the garage, I cocked an eyebrow at Old Red. He gave me a shrug and went back to drinking his tea. My ears were open extra-wide. If that boy laid a finger on my seeds, I was ready to whup him. Instead he came out with the mower.

Old Red gave me another shrug. "You fixing to cut the yard?" he asked Tommy.

"Yes sir," said Tommy.

Now, I know I should have felt thankful for Tommy at that moment, seeing as how he was doing such a nice thing, but I didn't. Instead I gave him a squinty eye and then went back to my gardening. Mr. Clancy had one of those old-fashioned push mowers that doesn't even have a motor, so when Tommy started, there was only a soft metallic hum in the backyard.

I could see him moving in neat rows. He'd disappear behind the house and then I'd catch sight of him as he turned at the fence and started walking back. He finished after a while, spraying the blades of the mower until they were clean and then putting that mower back in the garage. I was sitting on the porch by then, my legs draped over the steps. They were already deep brown from the summer sun.

"I'll be back next week," said Tommy. He picked up a piece of gravel that had been carried in from the road and rolled it in his hand. "Guess I'll be heading off now. " He cleared his throat. "Delia, are you ready to leave? I could walk you home."

That boy was one big pile of sweat, his blond hair plastered to his forehead. Freshly snipped grass covered his shoes and clung to his legs. He smelled earthy and green, almost like a thunderstorm.

I love the smell of thunderstorms.

"Thanks anyway," I said. "Old Red and I still have some business to attend to."

Tommy nodded. "Okay. See you tomorrow, then."

Old Red and I were silent as Tommy walked away. Before he turned the corner he pulled off his shirt and tossed it over his shoulder. He was thin and firm, like a good skipping rock. Not that I was watching.

August

"Wear something light!" I yelled in Mama's general direction as I got ready for church. Our house felt like an oven, even though it was still early and the heat of the day hadn't kicked in yet. Folks at church were going to be fanning themselves full speed during the sermon.

Mama went to church with me almost every Sunday. At first she went so she could say thank you to everyone who had helped with the house. That took months. There wasn't a person in Tucker's Ferry who didn't want to hear more about what *really* happened to her after she got struck by lightning. The old folks were especially interested in whether she saw a bright light or a tunnel or heard voices of long-dead relatives while she lay sleeping in that hospital.

Mama disappointed them every single time. "I don't remember anything," she always said. "There was a storm, and then I woke up. In between it's just blank."

Sometimes they'd invite us to dinner and try to trick her, slipping in questions where she wouldn't expect them. The first time it happened, I about choked on my potato salad. But it didn't faze Mama one bit.

"Pass the salt, please," they'd say, "and tell me about those angels." Or, "Listen to those birds, sounds like something you might hear in heaven, doesn't it, Mrs. Burns?"

I was just as interested as they were. I've seen those specials on the cable channels about folks who died and then came back to life. They always saw something. Some of them floated over the hospital room, clinging to those fluorescent lights, watching the doctors and nurses poke and fuss. If my spirit ever left my body and I saw a bunch of doctors cutting me open, I think I'd die right there. They'd be stitching me up, and *thunk*, my spirit would crash down and make a mess of everything. In the television shows, though, people told tales of seeing family or friends, those who had already crossed over to the other side. Then they'd hear a voice saying it wasn't their time yet. The light would fade and there they'd be, right back in the hospital.

Mama swears that isn't her story.

Eventually folks stopped asking. But Mama kept coming to church with me. In the middle of Sunday service, we passed this little clipboard down the pews. One by one, each person wrote their name on the pad of paper. It was the preacher's way of taking attendance, I guess. I liked seeing my name right next to Mama's.

"It'll be a good one today," I whispered. My legs stuck to the pew as we got settled into our seats. The choir was already practicing. When Preacher Jenkins was brimming with the spirit, he ordered lots of singing. Sometimes he'd have the choir sing quietly and he'd talk over them. When he did that it was powerful, more like watching a movie than being in church. The music would build, his voice would get louder and louder, and before long I'd find myself holding my breath, taking in every word. I wasn't the only one either. On those days I could feel that entire congregation throbbing with energy. Other times that music was softer than a baby kitten, and by the time he finished his story, half the church was dabbing their eyes with a tissue.

That Sunday, Preacher Jenkins started with a question. "Has God promised us a problem-free life?"

I didn't say a thing, even as the word *no* was rolling around in my head. The congregation was silent too. They hadn't been warmed up yet.

The preacher continued, "Has He promised us a life on easy street? A life with no worries, no concerns?" Preacher Jenkins walked across the front of the sanctuary, Bible in hand.

"Brothers and sisters, God has not promised us any of those things. What He *has* promised is that no matter *what* happens, no matter *how busy* He gets, no matter how many *other things* are happening in the world"—he paused and the choir hummed low—"He will not forget us."

Murmurs of *Hallelujah!* and *Praise the Lord!* and *That's right!* came from the pews.

"How many of you have ever forgotten to do something? Maybe you were supposed to get a new lightbulb at the store, or finish some homework?"

He looked right at me when he said that. I squirmed in my seat.

"We make to-do lists and we stick notes to doors and cabinets. There are times I even tie a little thread around my finger." Preacher Jenkins held up one hand, where, sure enough, tied around his index finger was a thin red string.

"Whenever I see that string I am reminded of something that matters so much to me, that is *so* important, that I don't want to forget it." The choir began singing a little louder. "But God doesn't need a string."

No sir!

The congregation was starting to buzz. I could feel it and sat up taller.

"God doesn't need a to-do list!"

Amen!

"And God surely doesn't need a sticky note!"

Hallelujah!

Then the preacher spoke real slow, as if he wanted each word to rain down on us and soak in real good. "Because God has engraved us on the palms of His hands."

The choir was silent. No one coughed. Not a single baby was crying.

"Think about that," said Preacher Jenkins. "He engraved us, each of us"—he walked down the rows pointing a finger at one person after another—"into the palms of His hands."

Mama was looking at her palms. There were dark circles in the center where the skin pulled and puckered from having been burned by the lightning. I stared at mine too. At all the lines crisscrossing from one side to the other.

I'd written on my hands before. Last year at school, when I was worried about passing a test, I'd taken a pen and written the answers to some questions on the flat part of my palm. I figured I could open my hand during my test without the teacher seeing, and have all those answers right there in front of me. But I got so nervous about the test and about the teacher catching me that I started sweating. Every few minutes I had to wipe my hands on my pants. Before I even got to the test, the ink on my hands had run together and smeared until all that was left was a blurry mess.

I reached for Mama's hand, and with one finger I traced the letters of my own name across the scars. She closed her fist over the word, protecting it. Then she did the same on my palm. Her name written across all those lines that told the story of my life.

With eyes squeezed tight, I tried to picture God's hand with all those names. Each one carved as if in stone. Even in the dark, even when He couldn't read the engraved letters, He could feel them and know that we were there.

When church was over we all headed to the fellowship hall, where cookies were waiting. The grownups gathered around the tall silver coffee urn, standing in line like they were waiting for gas at the station. Mae was on vacation, visiting her grandma, and Tommy was staring with these weird puppy-dog eyes that made me feel all squiggly inside, so I went to find Old Red.

I found him near the cookies, standing with Mabel Thompson. Mabel was about the same age as Mama, had never been married, and—if I believed the gossip at the post office—probably never would be, unless she found a man who loved cats. Mabel had sixteen of them. Mabel and Mr. Clancy were talking about the weather when I walked over and joined them. I didn't say a word, simply stood there, silently waiting for Mabel to leave so I could update Old Red about our seeds. I'd been putting the dried ones in jars, and there were now stacks in the garage just waiting for us to start selling.

"You have a good week, Mr. Clancy," said Mabel as she turned to walk away.

"You too, Nancy," he said.

"What?" I glanced up at him, my eyebrows squished together. "That was Mabel, Mr. Clancy. Mabel Thompson. You've known her since she was little."

Old Red nodded. "That's what I said."

Then Elmer Floggett managed to make his way over, dragging that lame foot, his one glass eye staring right through me.

"Morning, Redford," said Elmer. "And morning to you, Miss Burns."

I could feel it more than I could see it. Old Red tightened, the muscles in his arm went stiff, and his hands gripped that cane until his knuckles turned white. On his face was that same lost expression I'd seen when we were walking home from the bus. My chest felt tight as a button.

"Hi, Mr. Floggett," I answered.

I could hear Old Red breathe a quiet sigh.

"Mr. Clancy," I said, "you should see if your friend Elmer might be interested in some flowers." I gave Old Red a look, the kind where my eyebrows almost reach my hair. Then I smiled sweetly at Mr. Floggett, making sure to look at both of his eyes. Every person we met was a potential customer. We couldn't go forgetting their names or Old Red and I would never get any business.

Mama came up behind me and whispered in my ear. "Look over there," she said, pointing with her nose. "What *is* the name of that woman with that god-awful pink blouse? I know I've met her before."

"That's Mrs. Chapman," I whispered back.

Mama snapped her fingers. "That's right," she said. "Lizzie Chapman." Then off she went.

I turned back to Old Red, watching him as he spoke. He seemed right as rain, trading tales with Elmer about Tucker's Ferry as it was more than fifty years ago.

Everybody forgets names, even Mama. What we needed were name tags. Some of the church members had permanent ones they could pin on their dresses or jackets so visitors would feel welcome. But the rest of us didn't have a thing.

Name tags. That would solve everything.

I left Mr. Floggett and Mr. Clancy and ran to find Preacher Jenkins so I could tell him my great idea.

September

The Tucker's Ferry School Festival kicked off the first week of school. It was part carnival and part fundraiser, not to mention that it was a great way for the Fire Department to show off their trucks. The trucks were parked at one end of the fairgrounds, the sun glinting off all that polished silver. It cost a dollar to ride all over town with sirens blaring.

Mae and I wandered past the kiddie games—the duck pond, the Hula-Hoop Toss, and the Wheel-O-Fortune where kids traded tickets for a spin of the wheel. *Every spin a winner!* We watched a few kids spin, then walk away with a free balloon or a sticker.

"I used to love the duck pond," said Mae. "I could always pull the duck with the *L* on the bottom."

"How come I don't remember that?" I asked. "I've been coming to this fair with you since before we were born."

"Because all you think about these days is Old Red and those stupid seeds and Tommy," said Mae. She gave me a smirk.

I punched her in the arm. "That is not true and you know it!" And with that I chased her through the crowd, past the dunk tank where a long line of kids waited their turn to put Principal Young in the water, all the way until we got to the doughnuts. Mrs. Grey was there in her usual tie-dye.

"Mrs. Grey," I said, "might you be interested in any flower seeds? Mr. Clancy and I are officially in business."

"You bet I am," she answered. "Stop by the shop anytime and I'll see what you've got." She cocked her head a bit toward the doughnuts. "You ready to try your luck?"

"We are!" Mae and I shouted together. Then we fished in our pockets for a dollar and handed it over.

There really wasn't any luck involved in bobbing for doughnuts. It was sort of like the Wheel-O-Fortune—every player wins. Mrs. Grey tied fresh glazed doughnuts to a string and then hung those from a metal bar that had been made for chin-ups. Without using their hands, each player had to kneel, squat, or crouch and somehow get low enough to grab a doughnut in their mouth and take a bite. It wasn't as easy as it looked.

Mae went first. She hunkered down and picked one hanging from the middle of the bar, which I could have told her was a bad idea—too many other doughnuts nearby to get in her way. And sure enough, that's what happened. As she tried to bite down on that doughnut, which was bobbing and weaving and running for its life, others smacked her face and her hair, covering her with their sticky, sweet shine.

"I think that was a bite," said Mrs. Grey. She cut down the doughnut and handed it to Mae. Even I could tell Mrs. Grey was just being nice. While Mae finished off her prize, I stretched my neck side to side, swung my arms in big circles, and bent forward to touch my toes.

"You're not running the hundred-yard dash," said Mae, chewing.

"Don't talk with your mouth full," I said. "All I want to know is this, who is the champion doughnut bobber in all of Tucker's Ferry?"

I waited, bending to the right, my left arm curved over my head as if I was a teapot.

"I want to hear you say it," I said. "Go on, admit it."

Mrs. Grey had a hand over her mouth, but I could see her laugh peeking out the sides.

Finally Mae said, "Delia, you are the best doughnut bobber in our school."

"Thank you," I said, giving her a little curtsey.

But she kept on going. "In fact, you're probably the best doughnut bobber in all of West Virginia, maybe even the world." She threw her hands in the air. "The universe! The galaxy!"

By then I'd stopped stretching. I stood there with fists on hips, my lips in a thin, straight line across my face, and my eyes throwing daggers. "You done?"

Mae nodded, then gave me one of her best sugar-sweet smiles. I bet she got two cavities from that smile. Serves her right.

With my extra-large mouth, I managed to finish in about six seconds flat. As I stood up with that doughnut clutched between my teeth, Mrs. Grey still cutting the string to release it, I saw Tommy. He was standing with his back to me, sizing up one of the ball-throwing games. The kind with tall white milk cans where the ball is supposed to drop right in but never does, because the can rims are bent a certain way to make sure the ball bounces out. Last year I must have spent fifteen dollars trying to toss a ball in those cans. One of the prizes was a purple dog the size of Mama. I wanted that dog something fierce. Those stupid cans had me moping for weeks after that.

I grabbed Mae by the arm and pulled her in the opposite

direction, away from Tommy. Suddenly my stomach felt all jumbled. It was probably the doughnut.

When we heard the caller announcing numbers for bingo, we bought our cards and sat down. At the tables were small bottles of ink that reminded me of school glue. Except instead of a pointed tip with a hole on the end, these bottles had a stamp. Push it on the paper and it printed a red dot no bigger than a dime.

Mrs. Bennett, who was sitting one table away from us, started screaming and waving her arms like she was drowning. Her face was the color of spring beets. "Bingo!" she shouted. "Bingo!"

One of the helpers came running to check her numbers. "They better get there fast or she's liable to pass out," I said.

Mae and I were all business when our game began. It's easy to lose focus in bingo and then it's impossible to remember which number went with which letter. I was doing fine, though, marking I-18 and O-64 and all the other numbers that came out of that black metal cage, until Jackson Miller passed by with his friends. Jackson was a year older than us, but he made a point of knowing every kid in Tucker's Ferry.

"You watch out for those Millers," said Miss Martha one day after they'd left the post office. "Never met a good Miller. Meaner than spit, the whole lot of them."

From the corner of my eye I could see the boys laughing, not paying any attention to us, and then Mae filled in a whole row.

"I've got it! Bingo!" she shouted, jumping up, knocking her folding chair backwards, and causing a clatter. She skipped up front to check the numbers and select a prize.

Jackson and his friends walked over like they'd been planning to play bingo all along. Jackson took Mae's seat and the others stood at the end, as if they were his own personal cheering section.

"That's Mae's seat," I said.

"Doesn't have her name on it," said Jackson. He was taller than me, and wider. One of those boys the high school football coach was already drooling over. Mae came back with her new card, unsure what to do.

"Get lost, Mae," said Jackson.

Mae's bottom lip quivered.

I swallowed hard, knots forming in my throat. Jackson had a way of making people feel smaller than dust. Taking a deep breath, I glanced around the tent, and then I felt my eye twitch.

"Mrs. Watkins," I called. A gray-haired woman in the front turned. She smiled when she saw me. "Is that seat next to you free? Poor Jackson Miller wants to play bingo, but this seat is Mae's, so I was hoping he could sit next to you."

Well, there is nothing old ladies like more than sitting next to a young man.

"Come on up here," said Mrs. Watkins. "I'll move my purse and you can sit right down. I can teach you fifty years of bingo tricks."

Almost as if we were in church, others around the tent chimed in. *She's good, son, better get moving. There's an open seat here too. So nice that the young people are playing bingo.*

Jackson gave me a stare that could have fried an ant, but I just smiled as he walked away.

"Sorry, Mrs. Watkins," I said when Mae sat down. "Seems like Jackson decided not to play after all."

"Kids," said Mrs. Watkins, as if that explained every-thing. Then her eyes brightened. "Delia, I hear you're selling seeds. You'd best be stopping by my house when you make your rounds."

"I will for sure," I answered. Then I grinned. Word was already getting around town. Old Red and I were definitely going to need lots of seeds.

"Thanks, Delia," whispered Mae.

I put my arm around her and squeezed tight. The only person in Tucker's Ferry who was allowed to give Mae a hard time was me. And that was that.

We were walking around the games one last time when we ran into Tommy. He was standing in front of a wall of bal-loons, a dart in his hand. If he could pop three balloons in a row, up, down, or sideways, then the largest prize was his. The catch was that he only got three tries.

When I spotted a huge purple dog hanging from the prize rack, I couldn't help myself. "There's that dog again!" I said to Mae, grabbing her by the arm. "Oh, I wanted that dog last year."

Tommy ran his fingers along the feathers at the end of the dart. "I could win it for you." His voice was quiet, his eyes focused on one of the balloons.

"Really? Would you?" My voice bounced up and down.

Tommy gave me a smile that came out of his eyes and ears and took over his whole face. For a minute I didn't even see the rest of him. All I could see was that smile.

Apparently dart throwing is serious business.

I would have stood up there, no different than if I'd been

throwing balls at the milk cans, and tossed one after the other. But Tommy concentrated, taking one dart at a time and eyeing it from top to bottom. First he pressed the point against the wooden railing, straightening it. After he'd examined it six ways to Sunday, he wiped that point with the tail of his shirt, as if polishing it might make it fly faster. Then he took the feather flights at the end and fluffed them until they were smooth and even.

When he started throwing, his arm was a blur. I'm telling the God's honest truth when I say that I never saw anything like it before in my life. In seconds it was over, three balloons popped, one after the other, straight in a line. Tommy beamed. He nudged my arm with his own.

"Pick out a prize," he said.

For some reason that made me blush. The warmth crept up my face. With a shaky finger I pointed.

I clutched that purple dog in one arm all the way home. After Mae turned toward town, Tommy and I walked the rest of the way by ourselves. We didn't say anything, but my head was buzzing with thoughts. It seemed every single one of my senses was on high alert that night. As we walked, I could feel the heat rising off his arm, warming me. His breathing was shallow and so was mine, both of us skimming the surface. The tiny hairs on my skin stood on end.

Without even looking, I knew his hand was right next to mine. Somehow our steps began to match, our hands moving forward and back at exactly the same time. Then our fingers tangled together. It felt like the Fourth of July all over again.

October

Cleaning out pumpkins is disgusting. Mama used to do it for me when I was little, but she doesn't anymore.

"If you want a jack-o-lantern," she said, "I'll buy you the pumpkin, but don't expect me to help."

I was out on the porch, papers spread underneath the giant mess. My pumpkin looked like he was having brain surgery, the top of his head open wide while I scooped the stringy orange insides. My spoon scraped the flesh, tearing away one thin layer after another, until there was nothing left but a hollow shell.

With a thick black marker I drew a design on his face. Round eyes with wide slashing brows that angled toward his hook of a nose. Then I drew a snarling mouth with razor-sharp teeth pointing in all directions.

Mama joined me as I was making my first cut. She sat down on the wicker chair and bundled herself in a thin fleecy blanket. I pushed up the sleeves of my sweatshirt. The cool fall air made my skin tingle.

"The little kids will run away screaming when they see that," said Mama.

I grinned. "Probably." After a minute I added, "More candy for us."

Mama grinned. "Where's the other one?" she asked. "I bought you two."

"Down there," I said, pointing with the sharp end of my

knife to the bottom porch step. "That one's done already. He's drying."

Mama didn't get up but shifted in the chair so she could see him. "He looks happier than the one you're making now."

"Well, I figured Old Red wouldn't want a scary one."

I kept sawing away with my knife. The slashing eyebrows were even more terrifying once I cut them out.

"Old Red said he hasn't had a jack-o-lantern on his porch for maybe thirteen years," I told Mama. "That is just not right."

After I finished the second pumpkin, cleaned up all the papers and the guts, and set the spoon and the knife in the kitchen sink, I headed off to Old Red's. The smiley pumpkin fit neatly in my arms and I hugged it close, careful with each step on that gravel road. When I got there, the front door was closed. Old Red usually sat on his porch every afternoon, waving at anyone who might walk by. But I hadn't seen him at all that day. There was no hint of Rex either. I placed the pumpkin on the porch, close to the steps but underneath the awning so it wouldn't get rained on, and sat on the swing, waiting. After a few minutes I decided to check on my seeds.

Labeled jars, the black letters sharp against the white stickers, were lined up in rows at the back of Old Red's workbench. In each jar there was a small pouch. I'd made the pouches myself, cutting three-inch squares from a long sheet of cheesecloth. Old Red had watched me the whole time.

"Now place one piece on top of another," he said. "Then dump two teaspoons of powdered milk in the center."

I lined that cheesecloth up exactly, then measured the milk from a silver can. "What's the milk for?" I asked.

"Soaks up any extra moisture," he said. "Sometimes I even replace it come February, just to be safe."

Once the tiny mountain of milk was in place, I gathered up the edges of the cheesecloth and wrapped them tight with a rubber band. Then into the jars they went, like tiny sacks of gold. I shook a jar gently, eyeing the seeds to make sure nothing was sticking together. There was a muffled jangle as the packets hit the glass.

With my bucket and shears, I walked out into the garden. The afternoon air was warming in the sun, so I tugged my sweatshirt over my head and tied it around my waist. Then I clipped seeds and set them to dry, one batch at a time, tending them as if they were newborn babies. In a way they were. Life, asleep in a seed, waiting for a chance to grow.

After a while, when I'd finished with the seeds, I climbed back up onto the porch, tapping that pumpkin stem for good luck. Maybe Old Red had decided to shut the door to keep out the October chill. He might not even have realized I was there.

As soon as my knuckles hit the door, it swung open. Rex ran past, almost bowling me over to get outside. I watched that crotchety, half-blind dog barrel down the steps and race to the backyard. He came back a few minutes later, looking about as relieved as a dog could look.

I held the door open and together we stepped inside.

"Mr. Clancy," I called. The house was silent except for the ticking of a clock somewhere in the distance.

Even though I visited all the time, months had passed since I'd actually been inside. The last time was in early summer, when Mr. Clancy had invited me and Mae in for a glass of lemonade. We'd wandered around looking at framed photographs on the walls, listening to the clink of ice cubes as he made our drinks.

"Look at this," I said to Rex, my voice barely a whisper. "What happened here?"

Rex didn't answer. He simply stared at that room the same as me.

What had been neat and tidy was now a big mess. There were piles of mail, half of it opened, empty envelopes scattered on the floor. Bags and boxes lay across the couch. Flies were piled up on an old plate of food. It didn't look like Mr. Clancy's house at all.

I picked up the plate, shooing away the flies, and took it to the kitchen. That wasn't much better. A container of warm milk sat on the counter. I held my nose as I poured it down the sink. There is nothing worse than the smell of spoiled milk. Except maybe the taste of it.

"Where is he?" I asked Rex while I washed and scrubbed. "Did he go somewhere with Miss Martha?"

Then I picked up all those envelopes and made neat stacks of mail. I sorted the bills, the sales circulars, and the newspapers, and I tossed the stuff I knew was junk right into the trash. I tied off the bag and brought it outside to the garage. When I came back in, the screen door slammed.

"Who's there?" The voice came from the back of the house, where the bedrooms were. It was Old Red. He'd been there the whole time.

"Mr. Clancy," I called, "it's me, Delia. Are you all right?"

When he stepped into the hall, I almost didn't recognize him. He was bent over that cane like a withered tree, his hair a wild snarl of white. For some reason he was wearing two undershirts, both of them untucked from his wrinkled dress pants, as if he'd been sleeping in his clothes. He had a sock on one foot; the other foot was bare. Deep lines dug creases across his face.

Every now and then I take a nap on Sunday afternoon. If I start sleeping too late and then sleep for too long, I wake up all groggy and off-kilter. Usually I'm in a foul mood, too, as if my body is angry at me for having to get up at all. That is what Mr. Clancy looked like as he stood there. Completely off-kilter.

Old Red glanced around the room, his mouth in a firm line. "I've been meaning to straighten up." His voice was hard as a hammer.

"That's okay." I gave him a grin, then reached for my stack of yellowed newspapers. "I can help."

There was a long pause. That clock ticked like a bomb. "Don't need your help," said Old Red. The words almost echoed. "Clancy boys don't lie," he added.

I could feel my eyebrows tighten. It seemed an odd thing to say. As if he was having a different conversation with someone I couldn't hear.

"I don't mind," I said. "Really."

His voice was louder this time. "I don't need your help. Or anyone else's help, for that matter." He lifted that cane and drove it into the floor with such a smack it sounded like a rifle shot. I flinched, almost waiting for the pain.

"But—" I started.

"This is *my* house, and I didn't invite you in! Now get out!" His face twisted, those lines crossing each other in angry patterns.

I backed up toward the door. My heart pounded. When I hit the hall table, I let out a little yelp.

"Get out!" he yelled again.

When that screen door hit the frame, I was already half out the front gate, racing down the gravel road like I was running from the devil himself. My chest heaved. I didn't even stop until I got home.

Mama eyes went wide when I burst in. "What's wrong?" she asked. "What happened?"

"It's Old Red," I said.

And then I told her everything.

She listened real close. Now and then she asked a question, but mostly she was quiet, her eyebrows drawn tight over her eyes. When I finished she put her hand over mine. "We need to call Miss Martha," was all she said.

The two of them talked for what seemed like hours. Mama spoke in hushed tones, but words carried in our house. They floated up the stairs and through the vents, and billowed down the halls. Our house wasn't meant for secrets.

"I think we better call his son," said Mama. "He could get Mr. Clancy to the doctor."

Then Mama listened. "Mm-hmm," she said. "I've noticed that too."

Of course I couldn't hear what Miss Martha was saying, but I could figure it out pretty good based on Mama's replies.

"So you'll call, then," said Mama. "You've got the number?"

There was a pause. I sat on the stairs, my ears wide open. Suddenly I felt the way I did when Mama got hurt. Waiting in that emergency room for news I didn't want to hear.

"Call me after you talk to him," said Mama.

Dinner was quiet that night. Mama wasn't much of a talker anyway, and I didn't feel like keeping up the chatter. In the back of my head I could still hear Old Red's cane hitting the floor.

When the phone rang, both of us jumped for it. Mama got it first.

"It's Miss Martha," she said, holding one hand over the phone. Then she started pacing.

"You did," said Mama. She nodded at me. "Well, that's good."

Then there were a bunch of *uh-huhs* and *mm-hmms* as Mama held the phone to her ear.

When they finished up their call, Mama came and sat next to me on the couch. She wasn't much for snuggling, but I tucked myself in the crook of her arm.

"Mr. Clancy's son will be here real soon," she said. "He'll get this all figured out."

I closed my eyes as she ran a hand through my bangs, her fingertips light over my skin. Eddie Clancy was coming. Straightaway.

He was sure to make everything right.

November

After school I changed clothes, pulling on jeans, a sweatshirt, and some old sneakers I didn't mind getting dirty. Then I made my way to Old Red's. In the time since his son arrived, he seemed back to normal. I'd heard talk of doctor's visits and vitamins and some sort of medicine. All that was good. Medicine could fix anything.

I'd heard Mama saying something to Miss Martha about "good days and bad days," but I wasn't even sure they were talking about Old Red.

I pushed through the gate, which caught at the bottom on fallen leaves and branches. There was an empty garbage bin in the garage and I dragged it out. My gardening gloves were on the workbench, right where I'd left them.

Handful by handful, I gathered up what was left of fall. There were twigs and brown leaves, dried up flower stems, and some thin tree branches that had broken off and fallen into the yard during the last heavy rain. I dumped it all into Old Red's burn barrel in the backyard. It was a rusty old thing, with dime-sized holes punched in the sides to keep the air flowing.

Old Red came walking out as I was making my way back to the front yard. He had a thick brown cardigan over his usual dress shirt. I could see that he was wearing only one undershirt this time.

I'm not sure what happens to folks when they get wrinkly

and gray, but it seems their thermometer breaks. Ladies at the post office, the ones who come to gossip with Miss Martha, are always wearing two layers too many. It'll be the dead of summer and they'll be buttoning their sweaters up to their necks. If I had to guess, I'd say that's the first sign of getting old. I'm pretty sure that'll never happen to me. I'm always the one sweating, even when everyone else is fine. Sometimes it's a wonder I don't melt.

Old Red tugged that sweater closed. I waited, watching his face and judging his eyes, but today he seemed sharp as a tack. It was a good day. Suddenly I felt lighter, as if right there in the yard the trees themselves had gathered up all my worries in their branches and lifted them away.

"I saw you out front with the pansies and decided to join you," said Old Red. "The cold weather doesn't agree with my bones anymore. I get creaky as a rusty door."

The pansies were a sight for sore eyes in that garden. In that sea of wilted brown, those flowers smiled and laughed and waved flags in purple and blue and gold. Against the dismal backdrop, their green leaves shone almost emerald.

"How come pansies don't smell?" I asked. I'd sniffed and sniffed until those flowers were in danger of getting sucked up my nose, and still there was nothing.

"Well," said Old Red, "I know a story about that."

I grinned and the world felt good again. He had a story for everything.

"My grandfather told me that once, a long time ago, pansies had the most beautiful smell," Old Red began. "They grew wild then, so many dotting the fields they were like stars in the night sky." Both of us looked to the heavens, even though it was the middle of the afternoon. "And the people loved them!" Old Red continued. "They'd trample through the fields to pick those flowers, bringing bundles back so that perfume would fill their homes."

"So what happened?" I asked.

"Well, in getting to those pansies, the fields were ruined, the grasses trampled flat. And the cows who ate the grass in those fields began to starve."

"That's not good," I said.

"The pansies could see what was happening, sure as they could see the sun rising in the east," said Old Red. "And so they prayed."

"Huh?" I glanced up, my eyebrows arched. I hadn't seen that coming.

Old Red nodded. "They prayed to lose their scent."

I stared at those little pansy faces and thought about how courageous they were to give up something for someone else, to pray for it even. I'd given up little things before, a pencil, a cookie, and once, when Mama had taken me to the fair, I'd given my balloon to a little boy whose own bright red one had floated off above the trees. But I'd never given up anything that mattered much.

"And now they have none," I said, my voice barely a whisper.

"Once there was no perfume, the people stopped picking them, the grasses grew, and the cows became fat and happy."

We were quiet then, both of us staring at those pansies.

"Do you think they miss it?" I asked. "Their scent, I mean. Do you think they ever want it back or wish they'd never given it away in the first place?"

Old Red shook his head and started walking back toward the house, tugging his sweater closer to his chest. "I think they forgot about it the minute they finished their prayer."

As I raked and gathered the last of the leaves and twigs, I promised myself I'd try to be more like those flowers.

I was making another trip to the burn barrel when I heard the bang of a hammer. Sure enough, when I rounded the corner, there was Tommy. He was standing at Old Red's workbench, the flower boxes from the front porch perched in front of him. I'd been planning to take them down, and here Tommy had beat me to it. I rested against the edge of the garage, well behind him, and watched.

I liked watching him, especially when he didn't know I was doing it. Every now and then I'd hear him whisper. When I was alone I talked to myself too. There's comfort in hearing a voice when the world is silent. Sometimes he'd push the hair from his face, that floppy blond hair that I used to think needed a cut.

So as not to startle him, I gave a little cough.

"Hey there," I said.

My stomach fluttered a little when he turned and smiled. Tommy's smile makes his whole face brighter. Maybe that happens with everybody, but I noticed it most with Tommy.

"I saw you head this way earlier and thought I'd come help," he said, gesturing to the workbench.

"Thanks." My head cocked to one side. "How'd you know that was exactly what I needed?"

Tommy smiled again, setting the hammer down. "Because way back, when you and Red were planning, you told me."

It was as simple as that. I'd told him, and he'd listened.

All of a sudden, in that dim garage, in the middle of November, it felt like spring had sprung. I grinned all the way home that afternoon. I bet when Mama snuck in my room the next morning at six o'clock, which is the time I was born, I was still grinning.

I heard the door creak open and I woke to the smell of burning wax—that warm, toasty, half-melted scent. Then my nose picked up sugar and icing. I opened my eyes and there was Mama with my birthday cupcake. Once a year I get to have dessert for breakfast.

"Happy birthday, baby," she said, perching on the edge of my bed. The mattress sagged in her direction. "Come on, make a wish."

The world was blurry at the edges; I was still half asleep. Mama smiled and I smiled back. It's hard not to smile when you're going eyeball to eyeball with a frosted chocolate cupcake. I sucked in a breath and blew, then closed my eyes and made a wish.

Mama cleared a space on my dresser and set the cupcake down. "See you in a few minutes," she said. "I've got a whole batch of warm cupcakes downstairs."

Before she shut the door, she turned, and somehow a wrapped package appeared in her hands. "Oh, and I thought you might like this," she said.

The colorful paper was smooth to the touch. Long strands of curly ribbon tickled the soft skin under my wrists. I slid the ribbon off, then tore through the taped edge. Inside was a journal. The cover was made of navy canvas, the pages inside blank. *Everyone has a story—find yours. Happy thirteenth birthday!* That's what Mom had written on the first page.

"Like it?" asked Mama. Her eyebrows were raised, waiting.

"Love it," I answered, jumping out of bed and giving her a hug.

"Every teenager needs a place where they can complain about their parents in private." Mama laughed, then shook a finger at me. "Just don't fill it up too quickly."

I carried that journal around with me at school the entire day. In each class I'd open the cover, find the first blank page, then hold my pen over the paper and think about what to write. It was too nice to write just anything. It had to be special.

It wasn't until library that I finally figured out what that journal was really for. As I was searching through the racks, trying to find a title, Mrs. Hutchinson, the Tucker's Ferry Middle School librarian, noticed me carrying it. She put a hand on my back and whispered into my ear, "That looks like a good place for keeping memories."

"It does, doesn't it," I answered. I held out the journal. "The only thing is that I'm not sure how to start."

Mrs. Hutchinson had a gleam in her eye. "The beginning is always a good place." And with that, she moved on to help the other students.

I sat down at an empty table then, opened that journal, and without another thought I started writing. The words poured out of me. I wrote about Mama and the lightning, about the town coming to help and the fear that clutched me with sharp claws when Tommy fell off that roof. After that I wrote about Old Red and Dickie McDooley. Just thinking about those boys and that bus driver made me laugh.

The house was quiet when I got home from school. Mama was working the evening shift at the diner. I peeled an apple and opened the jar of peanut butter, then stood in the kitchen, my hip against the counter, dipping my slices into the thick, gooey brown. The calendar on the wall still said October. Mama hadn't flipped it yet. I wiped my hands on my pants, then walked over and turned the page, pushing the tack through the paper, making sure to get it in exactly the same hole Mama had made in the wall.

Turned out November was full of notes. Mostly mine. I'd forgotten I'd written them. There, marked in blue ink, it said, *Gather last seeds! Plant bulbs! Rake! Take down flower boxes!* And in capital letters, *PANSIES!* In Tucker's Ferry, pansies could live most of the winter if they were planted in the right place. I've heard that up north, in places that get colder during the winter, not a single flower grows until spring. That's just not right. If I ever live up north, which I probably never will, I'd have to live next to a florist. That way I could stop in and visit summer anytime I wanted.

Everyone has a favorite flower. Mama loves sunflowers, and Old Red is partial to his roses, even though he puts up a big fuss to make me think he loves all the flowers the same. For me, it's the pansies. I'm not sure why. Maybe it's because they're stronger than everyone gives them credit for.

December

Miss Martha had enough brown sugar in her kitchen to sink a ship. The table was covered in bags of it. Miss Martha didn't know how to cook anything in small batches.

"Oh Lordy," said Mae. "Here we go again."

"Better than vinegar," was all I said. Mae and I had helped Miss Martha make pickles before, and we'd smelled like vinegar for weeks.

According to Miss Martha, the most important part of the holidays had nothing at all to do with turkey or presents. "What everyone really looks forward to," she said, waving a wooden spoon at us, "is the pie."

Once we'd been aproned up, we went to our stations. There I stood, facing five-pound sacks of flour, while Mae cracked eggs and separated them, letting the whites drip off in one bowl and dumping the yolks in another.

"Meringue whips up higher with warm eggs," said Miss Martha as she buzzed about. "Yes it does!"

In front of me was a handwritten card, frayed at the edges, with the recipe for Granny's Pie Crust. "Follow that exactly," said Miss Martha. "Granny was my great-great-grandmother, and we've been passing her recipe down through the family for four generations."

I looked at the card, bent and stained. It had been in kitchens just like Miss Martha's for years, listening to ladies talk while they were making pie. It made me think of my seeds.

I picked that card up carefully. Me and Mama didn't have any recipe cards like that. Most of our recipes came directly from the back of the box of whatever ingredient we were using.

With a fork I worked that cold butter into the flour. After a while I thought my arm was going to fall off. Meanwhile Mae was whistling, happy as she could be, whacking those eggs upside the head.

Once I added the ice water, I squished that dough in my hand, working it with my fingers until it was one big ball.

"Now we dust the counter and the rolling pin," said Miss Martha, sprinkling flour and rubbing it across the wooden roller. "And out it comes."

She took the ball of dough, rolled it into a perfect circle, and began pressing it flat.

"Get started on another one," she told me. "We need lots of crust. Can't have too much pie!"

Even though we were just making pies to take to Mr. Clancy's house for Christmas dinner the following night, Miss Martha was having us cook enough to feed the high school football team. I mixed cold butter into bowls of flour for what seemed like hours. As soon as that was finished, she got me started with all that brown sugar.

"We're making pumpkin pie," she said, "but that's not special." She waved it off with one hand as if she was sending that pie to its room without supper. "These three other kinds can make a grown man beg for more." Miss Martha cupped a hand at the edge of her mouth, gave me a wink, and whispered, "I've seen it happen." Then she ticked those flavors off one at a time. "Caramel pie, butterscotch cream pie, and bourbon pecan."

"I guess they all need brown sugar?" I asked.

"And eggs," added Mae. There was a mountain of empty cartons behind her.

Miss Martha nodded. "And then we just mix in a little of this and a little of that and bake it for thirty minutes until golden."

I'm telling you, if heaven has a bakery, it couldn't smell any better than Miss Martha's kitchen did that day. By the time we finished I had a fierce hankering for pie. Miss Martha must have noticed, because she offered me and Mae slices of one of those ordinary pumpkin ones and sat us down with a fork and a glass of milk. I think ordinary must be in the eye of the beholder. It was the best pumpkin pie I'd ever tasted. Without even trying I could have eaten three more slices.

Miss Martha brought six pies to Old Red's house. One pumpkin, one pecan, and two each of the caramel and butterscotch. The meringue toppings were fluffy and white, the edges perfectly tinged with brown. Everyone oohed and aahed over those pies. I couldn't help but steal an edge of crust before dinner. It fell apart in my mouth and left a buttery taste.

Old Red's house was back to normal. Eddie had gotten it all straightened away when he arrived. There wasn't so much as a speck of dust on any of the furniture. Even the stale air had been replaced by the smell of roast turkey and gravy.

Every family that came brought more food. It's surprising the table held up under the weight of all those glass dishes. Mae's mom brought broccoli cheese casserole. She made the best one ever—it was almost all cheese. Mae's mom wasn't big on broccoli, or any other vegetable for that matter, but she did love Velveeta. A bag of fresh-baked rolls from the IGA arrived with Elmer Floggett. I coated mine with a thick layer of butter. Mr. Pete, who owned the hardware store in town, brought a salad. A real green-lettuce kind of salad. It didn't have any mayonnaise or fat on it at all. I'm not sure what he was thinking.

The Parkers weren't there. They'd driven to Ohio to spend the holiday with Tommy's grandparents. I have to admit I missed having Tommy around. Part of me kept wishing they'd show up in the driveway and pop through the front door, surprising us all.

I'd heard from Miss Martha that there were some women in town wishing Mr. Clancy's son Eddie would stay for good. I'm not sure how old he was. Older than Mama, I think, but younger than Miss Martha. He was single. And handsome. Which is why some of the ladies in town were buzzing.

Eddie Clancy was in charge of the turkey. Miss Martha walked into the kitchen every few minutes to check on it, but he kept shooing her out.

"I know how to cook this bird, so you just go enjoy yourself," said Eddie.

That about killed Miss Martha.

Mama and Mr. Pete stood in one corner of the living room, talking up a storm. Every now and then I could hear Mama laugh. It was a nice sound. Mr. Pete was sweet on Mama, but she wasn't ready to admit it. The way she told it, he just happened to drive past every week. It was as clear as day that he was working up the courage to ask her for a date. I was secretly hoping she'd say yes.

When Eddie announced that the turkey was ready, we gathered around the kitchen table, all those casserole dishes making my stomach grumble, and held hands. Eddie started.

"Thank you for this food, and for these friends, and now, let us each voice our own thanks."

I wasn't sure what he meant by that, so I opened one eye and glanced around. Mr. Pete was standing directly next to Eddie. He didn't seem troubled one bit, and without missing a beat, said, "Thank you for new beginnings." Mama added thanks for "children, both young and old," which made me grin. There were thank-you's for good health and good neighbors. Miss Martha said a thank-you for pie. I almost burst out laughing at that, and then she added, "Which makes us all remember how sweet life really is."

My palms started to sweat as it got closer to me. I had no idea what to pray for. And I didn't like praying aloud. I wasn't good at it. Everyone else's words always sounded better than mine.

I didn't even hear what the person next to me said; all I knew was that it was my turn. Frozen for a second, I opened my eyes and stared out the kitchen window. Then I said the first thing that came to mind. "Thank you for gardens." Which of course was about the most stupid thing to say, seeing as it was December and the garden was all but dead.

Old Red was last to go. I watched him through one squinty eye. His hair was combed carefully over his head, his button-down shirt tucked neatly into his pants, suspenders over his shoulders as usual. Nothing was out of place.

"Thank you for laughter," he said. It was almost as if he'd heard my very own thoughts earlier. And with that, Eddie ended with an *Amen.*

We all grabbed our plastic plates and utensils then, loaded up, and ate until our stomachs wouldn't hold any more. That was about the time Miss Martha started cutting pie. Mama groaned. Even Mr. Pete turned a sickly shade of green. Me and Mae lined right up. We'd been waiting all day for that brown sugar. I took a slice of butterscotch. Mae went for the caramel.

Before we took a bite, Eddie switched off the television. The room seemed louder without the noise. We all turned, our eyes on Mr. Clancy. He leaned on his cane.

"I'm glad you're all here," he said.

My stomach tightened. I knew that face. It was the same way Mr. Parker had looked when he was talking to all those doctors about Mama after she'd been hit by lightning. Serious and sad all at the same time.

I heard Eddie whisper, "It'll be okay, Dad."

When he finally spoke, his voice cracked. His eyes were wet and glassy. "I need to tell all of you something."

January

The bedroom window was open a sliver. Cold seeped in, icing over every inch of the room. Summer air was hot and noisy, coming with the call of birds, the snap of grasshopper wings, and the song of the cicadas, almost like a party. Winter air was quiet, more like a funeral, creeping in without a single word. I tucked the blankets tighter under my chin. My body curled into a ball, searching for warmth.

Even weeks later, I still couldn't believe Old Red's news.

"The doctors say I'm losing my memory." His voice shook as the words came out.

I heard Miss Martha gasp. Mama reached out and took her hand.

"The doctors don't know how fast it'll happen," said Old Red. He reached for the couch and Eddie helped him sit down. "It could be months, or maybe even years."

"Can't they give you medicine?" I asked. "To stop it?"

Old Red shook his head. "There isn't a cure."

We'd come back to our house that night with Mae and her mother as well as Miss Martha. We all needed the company, I guess. Taking in bad news is easier with other people around. Sitting together in the living room, we were silent as a prayer.

"Why would this happen to Mr. Clancy?" I asked.

"Why do bad things happen to anyone?" said Miss Martha. "There's no explaining fate."

"How will it . . ." Mae's mom stopped, her words quiet.

That scared me. Mae's mom was never quiet. She was born talking.

"How will he forget?" I asked. "How does it happen?" I sat on the couch, clutching the carnival dog to my chest.

Miss Martha dabbed her eyes with a handkerchief. "It probably started a while back. I've had other friends lose their memories. That Alzheimer's, it's a terrible, terrible disease." She took a deep breath, steadying herself. "At first, it all seems normal, forgetting a word here, or misplacing a pair of glasses there. Who doesn't do that?"

None of us said a thing.

"Then the names start to go," said Miss Martha, "and it becomes confusing to do simple things like start the car or get dressed for church."

"And it just keeps going," said Mama.

Mae's mom nodded. "One of my great-aunts had it too. As she lost herself, she started yelling at us kids in ways she never would have done otherwise."

I squeezed my purple dog and thought about Old Red screaming at me to get out of his house.

"Eventually he'll forget his own phone number and many of the people and places that mean the most to him. And then he'll even forget . . ." Miss Martha couldn't finish. She hung her head and cried, her shoulders sagging as if all the worry and care of the world had been clipped to her like a clothesline.

What would he forget last? I didn't dare ask. Neither did Mae. Instead we cried along with our mothers and Miss Martha, our shoulders sagging too. Even together, we weren't strong enough to hold up that one big problem.

"I just can't believe his memories of Rosalea might go," said Miss Martha. "Doesn't seem right."

Mae's mom handed us each a tissue. "How'd they meet?" she asked.

Miss Martha smiled. Her eyes were red, tears still glistened on her cheeks, but that smile made me feel better. The way the sun coming out after a big storm makes me feel better, even when the ground is littered with leaves and branches that need to be gathered up later.

"I bet they met in school," I said after I blew my nose. In some ways it was easy to imagine Old Red as a scrawny young boy. I pictured him like a darker, more suntanned version of Tommy.

Mae nodded.

"That they did," said Miss Martha. "Rosalea's family was well-to-do. They ran a general store. It closed down years and years ago, but when I was young my family went there all the time. I loved that store." She let out another sob. "They had the best-tasting penny candy."

"And Mr. Clancy was a farmer," said Mama.

"That he was," said Miss Martha. "Had been working that farm since he was little, right along with his family. They weren't fancy like Rosalea's, but they had thousands of acres of land." She turned to me and Mae. "Worse things in life than marrying a farmer, girls. A farmer's wife never goes hungry, I'll say that much."

"Her family didn't like him, did they?" asked Mae's mom. She dabbed at the corners of her eyes.

Miss Martha shook her head.

It was almost like we were watching one of those movies

on television where we all knew how the story was going to end, knew we were all going to be crying, and yet we couldn't turn the channel.

"Oh, he was taken with Rosalea, and she with him. But her family had this idea of her falling in love with someone more prosperous, like the local doctor. They wouldn't let Old Red enter their house. Thought that might keep them apart." Her mouth tilted down in a frown. "Know what he did?"

"What?" I asked. My eyes went wide, waiting to hear.

"He stood out in the road and recited poetry to her."

"Really?" My voice squeaked. "Old Red?"

I tried to imagine him, suspenders holding up his best Sunday pants, skinny as a rail, with hair that flopped over one eye, clearing his throat and calling out to Rosalea. It was the most romantic thing I'd ever heard. I hugged my big dog tighter. "Indeed he did," said Miss Martha. "Day after day, once his chores were done."

"Do you remember any of them?" asked Mae.

"Oh goodness me," said Miss Martha. "I haven't thought about those poems in years." She tapped her chin with the fingers of one hand, as if her memories were stored there and she was trying to knock one loose. "I know he'd talk to her about starry skies and red roses, because Rosalea would repeat it to all us girls, her eyes all dazed and dreamy."

"That sounds like something Old Red would say to Rosalea, since she loved flowers," I said.

"I don't remember it all, but I do recall the ending went something like this." Miss Martha spoke in her clearest voice. "*I would give the stars to you, if I had to walk ten thousand miles.*"

We all sat silently when she finished.

"Imagine," said Mama, a gauzy film over her eyes. "A man telling you day after day that he'd walk ten thousand miles for you."

I stared into my crumpled white tissue. No one could forget something that important to them. They just couldn't. My hand moved over the purple fur, the rhythm slow and steady.

We all hugged when it got late, our arms tight around each other, none of us wanting to let go. It was as if we might never see each other again. Or maybe that hugging filled up what the crying had let out.

When everyone went home, I sat there for a long time, even after Mama had gone to bed, wondering about exactly what it was that made each person special, different from all the rest. No matter how I thought about that, I kept coming back to only one thing. Memories.

As babies, we're born blank sheets of paper. Not a single mark. As we grow and get older, lines form, then colors and patterns. Before long that paper is all sorts of brilliant. Like a kaleidoscope, no two exactly alike.

Now, though, if the doctors were right, Old Red's paper was being erased. Bit by bit those lines and colors were disappearing. Before our very eyes, that paper was turning white again.

I'd had times at school, during tests mostly, when I couldn't remember the name of a place or a person, and I'd sit there tapping that pencil on my nose, trying to bring it to mind. One trick I had was to walk through the alphabet, starting with A. I'd think each letter to myself and see what sprang up. Another trick was to close my eyes and imagine my notebook. If I could see the page, then I could almost read the answer in my head, which sounds like cheating but isn't. Then there were times when neither of those worked. On those days, all it took was for Mae to give me the first sound of the answer after class, and *bam*, it popped out as if it had been waiting for me the whole time.

That's how it felt when I thought of my idea for Mr. Clancy. That idea popped out of nowhere, speeding by so fast, I almost had to duck so it didn't knock me over. I jumped from the couch and raced upstairs to Mama's room. "That's it!" I yelled, shoving open her door. With a leap, I landed on the bed. "I have a plan," I said. "For Old Red."

"I'm listening," said Mama, even though her eyes were closed.

"Okay. Know how there are times when whatever it is you're trying to remember is on the very tip of your tongue but won't come out? And then all it takes is the tiniest hint and there it is again."

A drowsy *Mm-hmmm* came from Mama's side of the bed.

"I bet it'll be the same with Old Red," I said. "We just need to have the right hints. The good thing is that Old Red has lived in Tucker's Ferry almost his entire life."

"And so . . . ?" said Mama, rolling back toward me. She pushed her hair away from her face.

"I'm going to collect his memories," I said, nodding. "Get his stories from everyone in town and write them down. If he starts to forget one, we'll simply pull it out and read it again."

Mama set a hand on my arm. "Now, Delia," she started, the words feather soft.

Those gentle words fell like iron weights. Mama's words

were usually stronger. The sudden softness made it almost hard to breathe.

"Don't say it." I stared out the window so I wouldn't see the expression on her face. "I'm good at fixing things. And this *has* to work."

I took a long breath, feeling the air sink deep into my toes. Then I shoved those iron weights off my chest. My eyes met Mama's, and I nodded. "It'll work."

February

I started my project on Old Red exactly the same way I did my projects for school, beginning at the library. I ran in like I'd been wandering the desert and that library was the only water I'd seen in weeks. My first stop was the checkout desk.

If there was something to figure out, our librarian, Mrs. Elvira Hutchinson, was the best person to ask. She listened carefully as I told her about my project.

"I'd love to help," she said. "I've got shoeboxes filled with old photos. Have one right back here, I think." She reached down to a shelf. "Brought it in for Heritage Day and somehow it stayed. You're welcome to look through the pictures. One of them might give you an idea."

Besides the shoebox of photographs, Mrs. Hutchinson had a story. It turned out she'd been best friends with Rosalea. The story she wanted to tell took place after Old Red came back from the war.

"I don't know what he did over there, or what he saw," she said, handing me newly returned books, "but he came back changed."

"Changed how?" I asked. As she spoke I loaded the books onto a cart.

"Well, he'd lost weight, barely more than a skeleton really, his cheeks all caved in. He'd been shot, you know, in the hip, which is how come he got sent home. That's why he uses that cane. They never did get the bullet out completely."

I'd never once wondered where Mr. Clancy got that limp. Maybe I should have. The whole time I figured it was just from being old, and instead it was from being brave. They don't have classes on bravery in middle school. If they did I'd have signed up. It would have been helpful to learn how to stare down what I feared most and not blink.

"What really worried us all, though, is what happened at night." Mrs. Hutchinson finished with the books, and together we rolled that cart through the aisles. We searched the numbers on the spines and then slid each book into place. It's satisfying to know exactly where something goes, to get there and find a right-sized spot just waiting for it.

"What happened at night?" I asked.

"That's when Redford would walk. He'd close the door without saying a word to Rosalea and he'd start pacing the streets of Tucker's Ferry."

"How long would he walk?" I said.

"All night," answered Mrs. Hutchinson. "He'd open up the door in the morning, and then, with the curtains wide, the sun streaming in, he'd fall fast asleep."

I tried to imagine walking in the pitch dark. Tucker's Ferry didn't have streetlights, and when the sun went down, on some back roads, if the porch lights were off, and the moon wasn't full, it was blacker than tar.

"What did Rosalea do?" I asked.

Mrs. Hutchinson plopped onto the reading couch in the middle of the room. I sat down next to her.

"She called everyone in town, and we took turns walking with him. Night after night, for an entire year, someone walked with Old Red. Walked and talked."

I thought of all those people who had come down my street, hammers in hand, ready to help with the house after I asked for help. They'd come to help Mr. Clancy too.

"What did they talk about?" I was thinking maybe he told them stories about the war. About the friends he'd lost or the places he'd seen.

"Well," said Mrs. Hutchinson, "mostly he talked about Tucker's Ferry. We'd pass a particular spot and he'd remember something he'd done there. He'd go on and on about Dickie McDooley, Elmer Floggett. And he'd talk about running. Oh, it was a sight to see Redford run. Before the war he was one of the fastest runners in the entire state."

"So the stories were happy," I said. My eyebrows knit together. "Why was he so sad, then?"

Mrs. Hutchinson shook her head. "I'm no doctor, but I think he was doing his best to remember every good or funny or happy thing in his life, so that he could forget all the bad."

"And it worked," I said. It was more of a question than a statement.

"Eventually it did," said Mrs. Hutchinson. "One day he didn't need to walk anymore. Started sleeping again at night. That's when we knew he was going to be okay."

Mrs. Hutchinson gave me a long list of other people in town to talk to. I folded the list carefully, matching the edges, and kept it in my pocket the rest of the day. Even when I was walking home, shivering as the cold air somehow found a way through my jacket and gloves, I could feel those names.

I pulled the list out and unfolded it the minute I got home. Creases divided the paper into small squares. I traced my finger over the lines.

When Mae knocked on the door I about peed my pants. She'd snuck up the front steps quieter than a cat in a snowstorm. I folded my paper quick and shoved it back in my pocket. It wasn't that I was trying to hide it from her exactly, more that I felt I needed to talk to each of the people on that list myself.

"Hello!" Mae was carrying a huge brown paper shopping bag. She plopped it on the coffee table in the living room.

"What's this?" I asked.

Mae pulled out carefully cut pictures from magazines, bits of crepe paper, and ribbon, arranging them on the table.

I groaned. Mae was on the Winter Wonderland committee at school. And the committee was in charge of planning our first seventh-grade dance.

"So the school gym is supposed to look like this after you're done with it?" I held up one of the magazine pages.

Mae grinned, nodding fast. "Isn't it fabulous?" She took the picture and clutched it to her chest, then twirled right there next to the couch, as if she was spinning in a fancy dress. "Everything will be white and silver, and when we hang all that crepe paper in long streams from the ceiling, they'll look like moonbeams." Her voice was full of dreams and magic.

I hated to squash it, but February put me in a terrible mood. When God was making the months I think February was a mistake, like a burp. There it was, small, dark, and prickly. It had absolutely no redeeming qualities.

"You don't think it will just look like the gym with stuff taped all over the walls?" I asked Mae.

We stared at each other.

Mae's eyes narrowed. "You drive me crazy sometimes.

Now stop complaining and help me make these flowers. I got the idea because of you, so I figured you were the best person to help."

Of course that made me curious. Which is exactly what Mae intended. In the bag were hundreds of thin cardboard flowers. They'd been cut carefully, each one slightly different. The blooms sat on tall stems that even had leaves.

"These are good," I said, "but they all look dead."

Mae reached back down into the bag. "That's why we have gliiiitterrrr!" She sang the last word, stretching it out and draping it over the room.

"Oh my," I said, although I could see those flowers, all dressed up and sparkling, the light dancing with them as they hung on the walls.

We decorated until I was sure I had glue and glitter in places where the sun don't shine. I was going to shimmer for weeks. Even with only the evening sun coming through the front window, that living room sparkled. Maybe that's what February needed every year. Glitter.

While we were cleaning up, scrubbing glue from the table, Mae poked me in the ribs. "Has Tommy asked you to the dance?"

I kept scrubbing, but I could feel my cheeks getting warm. "Not yet."

"Well," said Mae, with a knowing sound in her voice, "he will."

"It wouldn't be the end of the world if he didn't." The words crumbled as soon as I said them. I glanced up. Mae was standing there, one hand on her hip, giving me one of those *I don't believe a single word you just said* looks.

"Okay," I said, holding my chin high. "Maybe I do want him to ask me."

Mae grabbed my hands and yanked me toward the stairs. "Finally! Now let's go figure out what you're going to wear."

I had tried on every dress in my closet—which isn't saying much—when we heard the doorbell ring.

Mama called up the stairs a minute later. "Delia! Tommy is here to see you."

Mae squealed like a stuck pig.

"Shhh." I held my finger to my lips even though I knew there was no hope of Mae shushing.

"He's come to ask you!" She untied a scarf from her head and fluffed her hair in the mirror. "I'll get out of here, but call me the minute he leaves!"

I didn't bother to check myself in the mirror. My boring brown curls hung however they wanted to, no matter how I combed, brushed, or sprayed. For some reason Tommy liked them anyway.

"I'm just leaving," Mae announced as she waltzed down the stairs. She pulled on her coat and we loaded her up with those silver flowers. "Got to get more stuff done for the *dance*." She gave me a wink behind Tommy's back.

If it wasn't against the law, I might have strangled her right then and there.

March

The folks on Mrs. Hutchinson's list were more than happy to invite me in and talk. They'd settle me down in the kitchen, put a pot of water on the stove to boil so they could fix a cup of instant coffee, offer me a drink and a cookie, and help themselves to one in the process. Not one person started in on stories before we were all cozied up and had ourselves something to eat. And not one person looked at their watch.

That's the funny thing about old people: they never seem in a hurry. Mama is always in a hurry, rushing here or there or running late to something. Then she'll be yelling for me to get downstairs and grab my stuff, and there are times when she tosses me my shoes and makes me put them on in the car as we drive. I think old people have figured out that being five minutes late really doesn't matter much. Once, I overheard Miss Martha tell Mama that I have what they call an "old soul." Maybe she's right. I don't think being five minutes late matters much either.

The third people on the list were Mr. and Mrs. Williams. I'd met them at church before. They lived near CJ's Diner.

"Hello, Delia!" said Mrs. Williams when she opened the door. "Come on in, my dear, it's still chilly out there."

"Who was at the door?" shouted Mr. Williams from the living room.

"It's young Miss Burns," Mrs. Williams called back. "Turn off that blasted television and come on in here."

"What's burning?" Mr. Williams shouted.

She caught my eye and gave me one of those *There's no explaining men* looks. I grinned. Then I waited in the kitchen as she marched over to the living room to collect her husband.

"Oh, it's Delia!" said Mr. Williams as he walked into the kitchen. "Why didn't you say so?"

I thought Mrs. Williams might pick up the cast-iron pan she had sitting on the stove and crack Mr. Williams in the head. Instead she opened the cupboard and pulled out three cups. "I'm making coffee for us, dear. Would you like a cup of hot chocolate?"

"Oh yes, please," I answered, watching from the corner of my eye to see if she had the kind with those mini-marshmallows inside.

"Such a nice woman, your mama," said Mr. Williams as he settled himself at the head of the table. "Whenever I have breakfast at CJ's, you know she refills my coffee as soon as it's half empty." Then he motioned for me to come closer as if he was going to tell me a secret. "Without me even asking," he added. "Now that's good service, I'll tell you. Can't get service like that just anywhere."

I felt proud knowing he thought so much of my mama.

"We heard you were collecting stories," said Mrs. Williams.

I nodded. "For Mr. Clancy," I said. "It's sort of a gift."

"Before Frank here starts talking about Mr. Clancy, which could go on for days," said Mrs. Williams, "I want you to tell me about the school dance. The pictures in the *Tucker's Ferry Dispatch* made it look lovely!"

Just the mention of the dance made me smile so wide I

thought my cheeks might burst at the sides. Tommy had only stepped on my foot a few times, and when we went to get a drink at the table where the chaperones were sitting, Tommy laced his fingers through mine. Our hands fit.

"My friend Mae and I made all those flowers on the walls." I'd seen the photos in the paper too. The flash of the camera had made that glitter sparkle. Mae had been right all along.

"Did you go with anyone special?" Mrs. Williams asked the question as if it was just the two of us ladies talking, having ourselves a cup of coffee and sharing gossip.

I nodded again. "I went with Tommy Parker."

"We going to talk about dances all day?" asked Mr. Williams. He stirred his coffee and took another cookie from the plate in the center of the table.

Mrs. Williams folded up a nearby magazine and swatted him on the arm. "Sometimes it's as if you were raised in a barn."

Mr. Williams rubbed a hand over his arm. "Well, she came here for stories. And I've got more stories than a dog has fleas."

"Well, then," I said, "pick me a good one." I took another sip of hot chocolate—it did have marshmallows—and got my pen ready.

"Have you ever been to Lost Lake?" asked Mr. Williams. "If I recall correctly, it took us boys about half an hour to walk there, back in the day."

I shook my head.

Mrs. Williams chimed in. "They weren't allowed to go there. It was actually part of an old rock quarry."

I'd seen quarries before. After the company finished

blasting out whatever they were looking for, they left giant holes in the earth. Usually those quarries had chain-link fences all around, with signs warning *Keep Out*.

"There was a natural spring near that quarry that had turned that big, ugly hole into a beautiful lake. Of course we had to climb over rough, spiky rocks to get there, which was why our mothers didn't want us anywhere near that place." Mr. Williams pushed up a sleeve on his shirt. "See this scar?" He pointed to a long, jagged mark. "Got that at Lost Lake. Of course the danger added to the thrill. Us boys probably snuck out there once a month during the summer."

"Did you swim?" I asked.

Mr. Williams gave me a grin. It was the kind of grin a little kid might give after they'd stolen a cookie from the cookie jar. "We'd rigged an impossibly long rope to a tree that sat at the top lip of the quarry."

"Those stupid boys would swing out into the middle like Tarzan, doing yells and then flying off in crazy flips and twists," said Mrs. Williams. "It's a wonder they didn't all kill themselves."

"That sounds like fun," I said.

"It was," said Mr. Williams, gazing off into the distance. I could tell by the look in his eyes that he was reliving it right that second. Memories are powerful that way. They can bring a person back to another place and time and make them laugh or cry all over again.

"One day," said Mr. Williams, "Old Red decided he was going to try some sort of new trick. We made up names for all of them, things like the Triple Screwdriver and the Double Dog Dive."

I tried to imagine the whole gang of boys, all of them staring at Old Red as he clutched that rope swing. Each of them dripping wet in their swimming suits, clinging to the side of that quarry. The rocks slippery from the water.

"We urged him on, of course, so there was no way he could chicken out." Mr. Williams gave a low chuckle. "His hands must have been sweaty, though."

"What happened?" I asked.

"Old Red slipped off that rope before he intended to. He maybe got through one flip before he did a belly flop the likes of which have never been seen before, or ever will again, in all of West Virginia. When he smacked that water, it sounded like the crack of lightning. I bet they heard it all the way down at the capitol in Charleston."

"Was he hurt?" I once did a belly flop at the pool, from the low diving board, and my stomach was sore for days afterward.

Mrs. Williams cocked her head, her eyebrows shooting high over her eyes. "When they brought him back, I was sure he'd broken his ribs. We wrapped him tight with those stretchy brown bandages and then the boys snuck him back home."

"His mother never did find out," said Mr. Williams, taking another sip of his coffee. He sounded pleased by that.

I closed my journal, setting my pen on top.

Mr. Williams pushed his chair away from the table and tilted back until it stood on just two legs. "We'd had a great day up until that belly flop. We were laughing and swimming and jumping off that rope swing in the sun. I thought it was a terrible way to end the day. But know what Old Red said?"

I shook my head.

"He said, 'Even I didn't know I could do a belly flop that good.' We were half dragging him home, and he was smiling like it was the first day of summer vacation. I'll never forget that."

I thought about that belly flop all the way home, wondering how Old Red could take such a terrible pain and turn it into something so nice. I would have gotten angry. Then I'd have carried that anger around like it was a favorite blanket, gripping it tight.

I think maybe bad things seem worse when people are alone. When they can turn that bad thought over and over in their head, polishing it like a stone, until it shines dark and black. Maybe the key to making things better is being with other people. Little by little, smiles and laughter and hugs can chip away at any dark stone, even if it's as big as a boulder to start. Then finally, bit by bit, it shrinks until it's no bigger than a pebble, something that even I could kick down the road.

April

As soon as the nights got warm enough, I carefully tilled a patch of garden in front of our house. Then I mixed up a custom blend of seeds from my jars. Mr. Clancy kept his flowers in orderly groups, but I wanted something different. In my mind's eye I could see all those mixed-up flowers holding hands while they talked, sharing their lives. Sort of like the coffee hour at church following the service.

With the seeds down, a thin blanket of earth warming them, and the right amount of water, I sat back and waited for the sun to do its trick. Most flowers will start to come up within two weeks of planting, but it's a *long* two weeks. I checked on that patch of flowers every day after school, staring at the dirt unblinking, hoping to see some bits of green. When those first tender stems sprouted from the earth, I called everyone I knew to come take a look.

Miss Martha crouched down so low I thought she might topple directly over and squash all my hard work. Her hand was soft in my own as I helped her up, the skin loose like an old shirt that had been stretched from years of wear.

"Just think," said Miss Martha. "Those flowers are going to stand up and look around and wonder where the heck they are! They've lived at Old Red's for years, and before that his mama's house, and his grandmother's before that. These flowers have lived with the Clancy family their entire life!"

My face lit up. Those plants were like a newborn baby;

I couldn't keep my eyes off them. It was as if I half expected them to grow as soon as I turned my head, and I didn't want to miss a thing.

Mae tried to pretend, but I could tell she wasn't very impressed. "Good for you," she said. "Now what?"

"Well, now that I know the seeds will grow, I can package them up and sell them."

"Oh," said Mae. She sounded about as excited as if I'd just told her there was gum on the bottom of her shoe.

Tommy was a bit more encouraging. "There must be enough seeds to cover Tucker's Ferry twice over."

He was probably right.

"You know," said Tommy, "in the back of the garage, near the mower, Old Red has stacks of plastic trays for seedlings. You could grow your seeds in those. I bet you could sell each flower for at least a dollar."

I thought about that. The idea wasn't terrible. There were lots of folks too impatient to tend seeds. Mama was one of them. B & C Gardening could sell both seeds and seedlings.

I found those trays the next day. They were thin and black and reminded me of a honeycomb even though the shallow cells were lined up in four neat rows of six. There were enough trays to start almost three hundred flowers. I filled them all with dirt, selected my seeds, and got started.

Turns out I was right when I dreamed up our business idea. Heirloom flower seeds are special, and people knew it. I barely had to knock on a door and folks had their wallets open, waiting to buy some.

"I heard you were coming around," said Mrs. Myers, handing me her money. She lived halfway between Old Red's house and the elementary school. "I've been coveting these seeds for years. I know I shouldn't have envied those flowers, but I did!" She clutched the packets I'd made up, each one simply labeled with the flower name, color, and a rough date for planting. "Be sure to save some of those zinnias for Esther Barrett. She called me last night and told me to tell you that if I saw you."

Mrs. Myers cut me a slice of pie and made me sit down to talk. I should have brought Tommy along. He would have come in handy. Even though Tommy was no bigger than a rail post, he could put away more food than anyone I'd ever seen.

I'd already stocked up on a second batch of packets by the time I went into town. Judging by the wad of bills in my backpack, B & C Gardening was off to a good start. Mr. Pete bought sunflower seeds, even though he had seeds from a fancy company hanging from a wall in his store.

"Those are Mama's favorites," I said.

Mr. Pete didn't say a thing, but his cheeks turned the color of those cellophane-wrapped roses they sell at the IGA.

When I walked into Carmine's Canine Salon, it was as if Miss Carmine had been waiting for me all day. "I've got some photos for you behind the counter," she yelled over the whir of the blow dryers. "For your story project." She pointed to the middle shelf as I walked behind the register. "And I definitely want some of your flowers."

"I'll bring some seedlings next time," I said.

Miss Carmine needed flowers in front of her shop something terrible. There had been a tree there once, coming right out of the sidewalk and shading anyone who walked past, but it had gotten sick and the county had cut it down. They'd left a low, bare stump. Now it's the God's honest truth that there isn't much that looks sadder than a tree stump. There isn't anything happy about it.

Flowers would be a colorful memorial to that missing tree. I was certain the stump would enjoy the company. Plus, every time Miss Carmine looked out her front window, she'd be reminded of me and Old Red. I figured that was a good thing.

I pulled out the packets, my journal, and a pen. Then I eyeballed the shelf Miss Carmine had pointed me to.

Inside an envelope I found three pictures. They were all black-and-white. The first one was of a little girl. Her face was turned upside down, every bit of it frowning. Even her pigtails drooped. Her hands were clutched near her chest, a single index finger pointed up. Next to her was a rosebush.

As soon as the dryers stopped, Miss Carmine came and stood by my side. "That's me," she said. "I'd just pricked my finger on Old Red's roses."

I glanced at the picture, then at Miss Carmine, trying to find the little girl in her face. "Was it even bleeding?" I asked.

"Lord only knows," said Miss Carmine. "For a minute I thought that flower bush had bitten me. I was screaming bloody murder."

The second picture was of the young Miss Carmine and a woman. I thought the woman might be Miss Carmine's mother. They had the same nose.

"My mother was pretty," she said. "We didn't have any money, but she could make a dress out of a potato sack and you'd have thought she'd bought it in the store."

I jotted notes in my journal.

When I turned to the third picture, I knew exactly who it was. It was the little Miss Carmine and a very young Old Red. He was still wearing his button-down shirt, but the sleeves had been cuffed and folded up so his muscles were showing.

"He and Rosalea used to help us out," said Miss Carmine. She sat on the stool near the register.

I laid her three photos on the counter, side by side.

"One time, before these photos were taken, we had nothing to eat." Miss Carmine shook her head. "My mother struggled to put food on the table, and she knew the Clancys had that farm. So we drove over to their place."

"What did your mother say to them when you got there?" I asked.

"I don't remember exactly, but I know she was crying. The Clancys pulled us right into that house. Old Red asked Mother for her car keys, and Rosalea ushered us directly into the kitchen, where she began to cook."

"Was she a good cook?"

"Gave everything she made a good dose of bacon fat." Miss Carmine grinned. "So, yes, she was a great cook. We ate until our stomachs were bursting. It was like Thanksgiving in the middle of summer."

"And what was Old Red doing with your car?"

Suddenly Miss Carmine's eyes were damp at the edges, but the crinkles in her skin were happy ones. "He was filling it with food."

I stared at her. "What?"

Miss Carmine nodded. "He'd opened up the trunk of our beat-up Buick, which could have carried a good-sized boat, and he packed it to the top with food. There must have been hundreds of Mason jars. They were filled with canned corn, green beans, and new potatoes. There was strawberry jelly and an entire row of pickles."

"They had all of that in their garage?" I asked.

Miss Carmine nodded. "Everyone back then canned food. And with their farm, Rosalea put up more than most."

My mama didn't can anything. We bought everything fresh from the Pick-a-Bushel farm market, which wasn't much more than a shack on the side of the main road, or frozen from the IGA.

"When he closed that trunk, you know what Old Red said?" Miss Carmine shook her head as if she still couldn't believe it.

I waited, not breathing.

"He said, 'Bring those empty jars back, and we'll fill them up for you.'"

We were silent then. I closed my journal, trying to imagine that trunk stuffed with all those jars.

"Can I take one of these, Miss Carmine?" I asked, holding up the pictures.

She nodded.

I tucked the photo of Miss Carmine and the young Mr. Clancy between the pages so it wouldn't bend. That was such a great memory. I was sure he had to have that tucked away somewhere. And if not, well, I'd help him bring it back.

May

Tommy and I knocked on Mr. Clancy's door the Saturday before Memorial Day. We were planning to take him into town for an ice cream. He wasn't walking so steady these days, but we figured that with both of us there he could rely on us.

The door didn't swing open this time. It was locked shut. I could see Rex through the front window, sound asleep on the living room couch. Even though I couldn't hear him, I'd have bet a dollar he was snoring.

"Where do you suppose Old Red is?" I asked. "He's always home."

Tommy hooked his thumbs in his belt loops. "Mom says he barely leaves the house nowadays unless it's with Miss Martha. She's been with him a lot since Eddie had to go back home. "

"Seems strange he wouldn't be here, then," I said, giving the door handle another shake.

"He must have had a doctor's appointment or something," said Tommy. "Or maybe he went to the diner with one of his old school buddies."

I nodded. That had to be it.

Tommy reached for my hand and we walked through the garden and out the gate. "Come on, Mae is waiting for us."

Sure enough, Mae was standing directly in front of the drugstore when we got there. The red stools in the back were empty when we all walked in. The silver trim sparkled. Mack

Buckle was behind the counter, wearing a crisp white hat and apron. I'm not sure how he kept that apron so spotless. I could barely make a bowl of cereal in the morning without getting some sort of stain. It drove Mama crazy.

"Do you carry mud around with you?" That's what she asked me once at the Speedi-King Laundromat as we sorted the whites and the darks. I shrugged. Most of the time I was just as surprised as she was, wondering how on earth some of that dirt got there.

"Ladies first," said Tommy. He gestured to the stools.

Mae and I sat with a stool between us, and Tommy sat in the middle.

I'm telling you, Tucker's Ferry had never seen an ice cream feast like the one we had that day. Tommy had a mound of strawberry balls with chocolate sauce, sprinkles, and so many syrupy strawberries it was an island of ice cream surrounded by a red river. Mae covered her vanilla with broken chunks of chocolate and toffee, as if a bag of candy bars had exploded directly over her bowl. Even though strawberry and chocolate was my favorite too, I figured I could always taste some of Tommy's, so I ordered my second-favorite sundae, the Butterscotch Bomb. I usually felt sick after I finished.

"Here's to ice cream," I said, lifting my glass of water high. We tapped our plastic cups together and then dug in. Those long silver spoons half disappeared into all that ice cream.

"Only two more weeks of school," said Tommy.

Mae nodded. "I can't wait for summer." Then she shoveled in more cookies.

Thinking about hot weather made me think about water. "Either of you ever heard of Lost Lake?"

Mae and Tommy mumbled a *Nuh-uh.*

It was hard to believe that such a fun-sounding place had been kept secret for so long. Maybe the quarry people had come along and closed it up after they found kids swimming in it. I'd have to see if Old Red knew.

When our bowls were almost empty and the three of us were starting to slow down, Miss Betty, who'd been running the drugstore for as long as I could remember, yelled back to where we were sitting. "Mack," she called in her sandpaper voice, "you seen Old Red Clancy in here today?"

My ears perked right up at that. I swiveled on my stool and leaned so I could see her. Miss Betty lifted up the telephone and spoke into the receiver.

The hairs on my arm stood on end. I glanced at Tommy and Mae, then set my spoon down on the counter. It seemed as if my hand was moving in slow motion. I climbed off my stool and walked toward the front of the drugstore, past thousands of little pills stored in tiny bottles wrapped in cardboard boxes, none of which could do anything to cure the sick feeling I had in the pit of my stomach.

"Miss Betty," I said. "What's happened to Old Red?"

"Probably nothing, my dear." She glanced up from the register. "Miss Martha's looking for him, is all." The look in her eyes didn't match her words. Eyes aren't good liars.

I ran back through the aisle, almost knocking over a wire rack of reading glasses at the end. Tommy reached out and steadied it. "Whoa," he said. "You okay?"

"It's Mr. Clancy," I said. "Something's wrong. I can feel it." Deep in my pocket were a few crinkled dollar bills. I tossed them on the counter toward Mae. "This should cover mine," I said. Then I turned and raced out of that store, trying to run faster than my fear.

No one was sitting on the porch when I got to Old Red's house. Everyone was standing around, shifting their weight from one foot to the other and wringing their hands, the way people do when they're worried. Worry doesn't like sitting still. I noticed that in the hospital when Mama was there. Worry likes to be up and moving.

"What's happened?" I asked as I was coming through the gate. My breath came in short spurts, as if I'd gone from one goal post to the other down the football field at school.

"We can't find Mr. Clancy," Mama said, her voice hushed.

"What does that mean?" I said. "Where is he?" My eyes darted across all the faces there. Miss Martha, Mrs. Parker, Mr. and Mrs. Williams, and Preacher Jenkins. People called the preacher only when they felt the need for prayer. Seeing him there should have made me feel better, but it didn't.

Miss Martha was the first to answer. "I was supposed to pick up Old Red today at two-thirty. We'd been talking about it all week."

"When she got here," said Mrs. Parker, "he was nowhere to be found. And his truck was gone too."

Mr. Clancy's truck was always in that garage. The hole it left was dark and empty. I walked inside, breathing in that familiar scent of oil and dirt and metal. Across the shelf on the left I touched each jar of seeds, tapping them on the top. Feeling them there calmed me.

"He'll be okay," a voice whispered behind me. I knew that voice. When I turned, there was Tommy.

"I hope so," I answered.

I'd never said it aloud, never told a soul, but I'd sort of adopted Old Red as my very own grandpa. He didn't have any grandchildren and I didn't have any grandparents. I guess we were both orphans in a way. We needed each other.

When we came out, everyone was standing by the front door. Miss Martha was fussing with the lock. "I've got a spare key," she said. "I think we better see if he left a note."

Tommy and I were the last ones in. Mama was already on the phone. She was standing in the kitchen, dialing number after number from her little black phone book. "Hi there, Mrs. Watson, this is Mrs. Burns. I'm wondering if by chance you've seen Mr. Clancy."

She nodded, listening to the words on the other end. "Okay, thank you. You have a great night."

Mama must have called every single family in Tucker's Ferry. I was straightening the living room when a flash of silver caught my eye. I turned, and there, through the picture window, past the porch and the garden, was a police car. And directly in front of that car was Old Red's truck.

We all ran outside, coming one after the other through the front door. I barreled down those steps and through the gate, grabbing Mr. Clancy before he had a chance to take two steps down the walk.

"We were worried about you." The words rushed out.

"I just wanted to go to the farm market," said Old Red. "Got to thinking about strawberries and decided to get some."

"Let me help you," said Tommy. He held out an arm for Old Red so he could steady himself on both sides, then walked him up to the porch.

"Found him more than thirty miles away in Putnam County," said the officer.

"Don't know how I ended up all the way over there." Mr. Clancy shook his head. "I've driven to the farm market my whole life."

Old Red's hair was a mess. I noticed his shirt had been buttoned wrong too, so that one side was higher than the other, the collar tilted. And his right shoe was untied. He reminded me of a little boy.

I kneeled down and retied the laces. Then I sat next to Old Red on that porch swing and fixed his buttons. My fingers trembled against the thin cotton. I kept my face turned down, not wanting him to see my worry.

When Mama and Mrs. Parker walked that officer back to his car, they spoke softly so their voices didn't carry.

"I'd recommend that he not drive anymore," was all I heard the officer say.

June

Eddie, Old Red's son, came back the following Friday.

"He'll be here for a week or two, just long enough to get things settled," said Mama. She locked the front door, closing us in for the night.

Settled wasn't a word I wanted to hear. Settled is what happens when what a person really wants isn't possible. Settled means everyone ends up a little bit unhappy.

"What's going to happen to Old Red?" I asked.

Mama sat down on the couch. I snuggled close until she had no choice but to wrap an arm around me. With one hand she stroked my hair. I closed my eyes and tried not to think sad thoughts.

"I'm not sure," said Mama. "But I imagine Eddie may need to arrange for Old Red to go to a special kind of home. A place where there are people who can watch out for him all day."

"Why can't we help?" I asked. "Why can't he stay here with us? I can keep an eye on him this summer."

Mama rested her cheek on my head. "I know you want to help. Over time, though, Mr. Clancy will need more than we can give. You'll go back to school, I have to go to work, and then what?"

I didn't have an answer for that. But in my mind's eye, all I could see was Mr. Clancy being the first one to stand up in church when I asked for help. He was the first one.

We sat like that for a little while, me tucked into Mama, her arms wrapped around me. I could feel her breathe, the rhythm steady.

"Is he going to die?" I asked after a while. I pulled away so I could look into Mama's eyes. I swallowed hard, my throat dry.

"Not for a long time, most likely," said Mama. "The problem is that he can't live on his own anymore."

"It won't be the same with Old Red gone, will it?" I already knew the answer.

Mama stared off into the distance for a minute. I could see the wet shine in her eyes. My own stung at the corners. When she looked at me her face was crumpled. Then she shook her head.

We both cried then, holding on to each other like we were riding out a storm. The crying came in waves. I'd think about one of Old Red's stories or something we'd done together and my soul would ache. Ache with a terrible, squeezing pain.

When our tears ended, Mama unwrapped me and pushed herself up from the couch. "How about I get us some toast with honey."

I could hear her in the kitchen, opening the utensil drawer, then popping the bread into the toaster.

My great-grandparents believed honey could cure any ill, but eating that toast didn't make me feel any better. I don't think Mama added enough honey, because I had a hard time getting it down.

I walked to Old Red's house the next day. I'm not sure what I expected to see, but there he was, sitting on the porch as usual. Rex was lying near his feet, sound asleep.

"Morning," I said as I walked through the gate.

"Morning to you, Miss Delia," he answered. "Come join me."

I sat down next to him on the swing, and we both gazed out toward the road. My eyes skimmed over the garden, which was already blooming. Flowers could almost always cheer me up, but that day they didn't.

I set my hand on Mr. Clancy's. They had been big, strong hands once. Now the knuckles were gnarled. His skin was speckled with dark spots, either from age or from the sun. And it was soft, but a different kind of softness than mine. His skin felt almost tissue-paper thin.

"Mr. Clancy," I said, "I was wondering if you'd like to walk with me to the creek."

I knew we'd have to go slow, but the creek was calling to me that day and I had a feeling I was supposed to bring Old Red.

He grinned. "I'd like that."

I went inside to tell Eddie where we were going. He was sitting on the edge of the couch, hunched over the coffee table and sorting through a mess of papers. The phone sat in front of him, its long cord twirled across the floor. His face was grim. I had a notion he was getting things settled, just as Mama had said.

Eddie nodded when I told him our plan. "Just be careful."

"I will," I said. Then, for some reason, before I walked out the door I turned back to Eddie. "I love him too." My voice caught at the end. Then I pushed through that screen door, not waiting for him to answer.

Together, Old Red and I made our way down the gravel road toward the path that would lead us to the creek. Rex stayed a few paces behind, stopping to mark the electric poles along the way. We walked in the center of the tire tracks where the road was smooth and bare. I gave Old Red my arm. With each step, I could feel him lean, using me as a second cane.

Once we turned onto the path, the water tumbled and bounced near our feet, urging us forward. "Smell that?" I asked. The air was thick with the scent of honeysuckle. White and yellow blossoms dotted the bushes as far as my eyes could see.

Old Red stopped, then lifted his face into the air and sniffed. I waited for a smile to wash over him. That's what happens when most people breathe in honeysuckle. The warm, sweet scent is almost like melted sugar. It's the kind of smell that makes worries fade, at least for a little while. When I stayed at the Parkers' after Mama's accident, the scent of those honeysuckles drifted up to my room, calming me to sleep as gentle as a lullaby.

The smile never came to Old Red. Instead, I watched as confusion filled his eyes. "Delia," he said, "I can't smell anything."

I took a deep breath, making sure the wind hadn't shifted. It hadn't.

"You must be getting a cold," I said. "My nose never works right when I have a cold." I tried to sound cheerful, but I bit my bottom lip between my teeth after the words came out. I had a feeling that right then and there, with me standing at his side, Old Red's life had just been erased a little more.

"Must be," he said.

We walked to the end of the path and came to the place in the creek where there was a pool. When it got too hot to do anything else, it was the one place where Mae and Tommy and

I liked to come. It wasn't wide, but it was deep enough for us to go under and have a good splash. Mr. Clancy and I sat down on the weathered bench. Rex was already sprawled out in the dirt next to it, as if the short walk had done him in.

I bent over and picked up some rocks. Then I handed a few to Old Red. Together we tossed them in the water, watching the rings grow wider and wider until the surface was calm again.

"I think you're officially the president of B & C Gardening now," said Old Red.

"I don't know anything about being a president," I answered.

"Well," said Old Red, "I never used to know anything about gardening either."

We both laughed.

When he spoke again, his voice was low. "But here's the thing. I'm only going to let you be president if you promise to come visit and tell me how the sales are going."

I looked directly into his blue eyes when I answered. "Promise," I said, crossing my finger across my chest.

Rex sat up and yawned, then lay back down with his head on his paws. The three of us listened to the cicadas and the birds and the song of that creek as it danced with the rocks.

"Mr. Clancy," I said, "can I ask you a question?" The words came out slowly, carefully. Half of me was afraid to speak them out loud.

He patted my hand. "Always."

I wrapped my fingers around his and squeezed. "Are you afraid?"

We looked at each other then. I mean *really* looked. It

almost felt like I could see his soul and he could see mine.

He didn't answer for what seemed like forever. Then he nodded. "Who will I be?" he asked. "If I don't remember my life?"

I didn't have an answer for that, but I held on tight to his hand. I knew exactly what he meant. Memories are what makes each person different. Even me and Mae could go to the exact same school carnival and leave remembering all the sights and sounds in completely different ways.

"How can a person forget all the things and the people that are most important to him?" A tear fell from the corner of Mr. Clancy's eye, leaving a trail down his cheek.

I put my arms around him and pulled him close. He tucked his face into the crook of my neck, the way I sometimes did with Mama when life was too heavy for me to carry on my own.

"Oh, Mr. Clancy," I said. "It doesn't mean they didn't matter to you."

"I know," he said. "But that's how it's going to feel."

One other question swirled in my mind. I didn't want to ask it. But at the same time I did. I had to know. "Will you forget me too?" My voice squeaked when I said it.

Old Red clutched me tight. Then he pushed back my curls and gave me a soft kiss on my forehead. "Delia," he said. "I will always remember you in here." He pressed my hand to his chest.

I think my heart broke in half right then.

The two of us sat there on that bench, hugging each other and crying. I'm not sure, but I think both of us were hoping the same thing. That this was a day we'd never forget.

July

Old Red moved to a place called Riverdale not more than a week after we'd gone to the creek. It was the kind of place that specialized in taking care of folks with problems like his. I'd seen the pictures on the brochure Eddie had given us with the address. I didn't think it looked near as nice as Old Red's real house.

Before he left, a bunch of folks went over to say goodbye. I didn't. Part of me hoped that if I didn't say it, he wouldn't leave.

Mama went, and so did the Parkers and Miss Martha.

"Old Red asked where you were," said Miss Martha the next time I saw her at the post office. I could hear the scolding in her voice.

When I walked home after that, it felt as though I went a million miles, dragging my heart behind me on a string. My chest felt bruised and swollen, with bits of gravel stuck in places I couldn't quite reach.

I think maybe it was the flowers that made me stop feeling sorry for myself. The sunflowers in our gardens were tall that summer, their faces bigger than a plate. No matter the weather, those flowers smiled and shone and greeted everyone with a big hello. I couldn't help but look at them and see the thousands of seeds I'd have once they dried. With Old Red gone, I had double the work to do for B & C Gardening.

When Mama saw me pack up Old Red's stories and slip

them in my backpack, she knew exactly where I was headed. Riverdale wasn't that far, maybe twenty minutes by bike.

"He'll be happy to see you," was all she said.

My bike was still lying on the grass in the front yard, right where I'd left it. I lifted it up and squeezed the brakes a few times. Then I pedaled.

Riverdale looked better in person than it did on the brochure. It didn't feel like the hospital Mama had stayed at after the lightning. That's what I'd been expecting. Doctors and nurses, charts and bright lights, and buzzers sounding from every direction.

Inside, Riverdale felt more like a home. There was soft music playing, plush couches set around a fireplace, and a big dining room with real wooden tables and chairs.

"Well, hello there," said a young woman. "I'm Lily." She pointed at the name pinned to her dress. "I'm guessing you're here to see someone."

I nodded. "His last name is Clancy," I said. "We all call him Old Red."

She grinned. "We call him Old Red, too. Follow me and I can lead you to him."

With each door we passed, each corner we turned, I could feel my breath coming faster. I'd heard Miss Martha telling Mama that Old Red had aged ten years as soon as he got here. I wasn't sure what she meant by that exactly.

Then, without warning, there he was, looking just the same to me. Well, maybe he looked more tired than usual, but I never slept well in new places either. We turned into a bright room splashed with sunshine. It was bigger than I expected, like a bedroom and a living room all squished into one.

"Well," he said, sounding just like he was standing on his front porch, "look what the cat drug in."

"Hi, Mr. Clancy," I said.

Lily excused herself. "Ring the front desk if you need anything." I wasn't sure if she was talking to me or Old Red.

It felt strange when she left. At home we had the flowers and the porch swing and Rex. We had a routine. Here, everything was different. My eyes fixed on the couch and the bed and the lamp. I shifted my weight from foot to foot. Then I glanced at Old Red.

He was smiling. Smiling the same way he would have if I'd seen him the day before. "Come here and give an old man a hug."

He didn't mention my not coming to see him the day he left. With just that hug, the guilt lifted off my chest. Preacher Jenkins said once that being forgiven is like having all the worst bits of yourself stuffed into a balloon and then having that balloon set free. My balloon was floating somewhere far over Tucker's Ferry and headed out of town.

As I hugged Mr. Clancy, I noticed lots of little things. The scent of his musky aftershave, the scratch of his gray whiskers on my cheek, and the way his suspenders never lay quite evenly on his shoulders. I'm not sure why, but when a person expects something to last forever, they don't notice the little things. It's only when the clock is ticking that all those little things add up and become bigger.

"I've got a present for you," I said, shedding my backpack.

We sat together on the couch. Out came my journal, a stack of papers, and some photographs.

"What's all this?" he said. "Wait a minute." He pulled a

picture from the top. "This is the Brier River, where I was . . ." I could see him struggle for the word.

"Baptized," I said.

"Right. Silly to forget such an important word, isn't it. Have I ever told you about that?"

I'd heard the story a dozen times, but I shook my head anyway, then tucked a leg under me, ready to listen.

"It was cold that day, and Preacher Charley—he was the one before Preacher Jenkins, see—well, he wasn't taking any mercy on me." Old Red's cheeks shone pink as he talked. His face was thinner than before too. I wondered if they were feeding him right. "Dunked me completely under. I was frozen for a week. Couldn't feel my left pinkie toe after that. Some people give their soul to the Lord, I gave my soul and my left pinkie toe."

I laughed.

"You know," I said, "Elmer Floggett told me that same story about you, Mr. Clancy." I pulled it from the stack and matched it to the photograph. "He said you cried like a baby that day."

"He's probably right," said Old Red. Then he shook his head. "Me and Elmer were good friends growing up. I'd bet my right leg that he's going to outlive his glass eye."

"He's not the only one telling stories about you. See? I've been writing them in my journal"—I flipped through my book—"but then I got to thinking how you might like them too, so I copied them onto these papers." I grabbed the roll of tape from my bag. "I thought we could hang them up. Make it feel a little more like home."

"Or like the post office," said Old Red. "Full of gossip."

We hung the pictures and the stories together, thinking about where each took place in relation to the others so we could put them in the right spot. It was like creating a map of Tucker's Ferry and Old Red's life all rolled into one. Maybe when a person lives in a single place so long, that's what happens—their histories get woven together.

"Where's my cane?" he asked. "I'd like to show you something."

Walking through that hall was no different from walking down the street at home. Old Red was stopping every three steps to talk and greet and visit.

"How are you doing today?" he called to an elderly woman, raising one hand in a sort of wave. "Good afternoon," he said to one of the Riverdale employees walking past.

After what seemed like an hour, we got moving faster. We turned down different corridors and finally stopped in front of a door with a tiny metal placard inscribed CHAPEL.

Old Red had brought me to church.

It wasn't a big room. There were a few rows of pews, a small pulpit, and a font for the kind of baptisms where the pastor dips his hand in the water and then marks the person's head. Behind the pulpit, high on the wall, was a stained-glass window of a butterfly rising from its cocoon. Streams of gold, red, green, and blue crisscrossed the room. Tiny bits of dust floated like stars, sparkling in the light. Old Red and I were the only people there, but somehow, even in the quiet, it didn't feel lonely. We were wrapped in colors.

"Here's what I wanted to show you," he said.

He pointed to a side wall. On it hung what looked like a rag rug. Scraps of fabric no bigger than a stick of gum had been tied in knots to a white canvas woven so that the threads formed tiny open squares. Each piece of knotted fabric left the ends sticking out in the front.

It wasn't finished. There were still open sections, bare and white.

"What is it?" I asked. Seemed odd to me that there would be a rug hanging on the wall.

"It's for prayers," said Old Red. He reached into a small box on the table beneath the rug and pulled out two pieces of fabric. "Here. We can each do one."

I fingered the material, which was a pale yellow calico. "What am I supposed to do exactly?"

"Say a prayer and then . . ." Old Red made tying motions with his hands. "I like coming here and touching all these prayers." He ran his fingers over that rug. "Usually prayers are invisible, but coming here lets me see them all in real life."

I closed my eyes and held tight to that small scrap of cloth. When I was finished, I picked a square in that wide-open white space and tied my fabric on. Old Red tied his right next to mine.

He nudged me with his elbow. "What'd you pray for?"

"I can't tell you!" I said. Telling a prayer seemed like telling a birthday wish, and there isn't a person alive who doesn't know that not-telling is the only way to be sure it comes true.

"Was it about Tommy?" he asked.

"No!" I could feel the blush rising in my cheeks even as I was saying it.

Old Red grinned. "Wanna know what I prayed for?"

"Sure," I said.

"Well, there's this nurse here. Can't remember her name.

But she wears the most lovely gardenia perfume. You know, that's one of the only things I can smell now. Gardenia. Makes me feel like I'm back in my garden. Anyway," he said, "I prayed she'd stop by tonight."

"That's nice." I grinned, thinking of all the time we'd spent together in his garden.

"And while she's there," he said, a gleam in his eye, "I wouldn't mind a kiss on the cheek."

August

The blow dryers were going full steam at Carmine's Canine Salon, located directly below Mae's apartment. We could hear them humming. The air in the apartment was about four hundred degrees. If the sun hadn't been blocked by the curtains, it would have felt like we were on broil.

Mae and I worked for Miss Carmine once, and it was about the longest day of my life. The smelliest, too. I was not cut out for the doggie salon business. Selling flowers is a lot easier, if you ask me.

By now, everyone in town knew about B & C Gardening. Between drying seeds, writing up orders, and delivering seedlings, I barely had time for anything else. I was keeping track of every dime we made, marking it down in my book so I could give Mr. Clancy his half.

"What do you think of this?" asked Mae. She turned from the mirror where she'd been staring at herself, making pouty faces, and twisting her hair into fancy shapes.

"What's wrong with a regular old ponytail?"

Mae gave me one of her stares. The kind where her eyes went all squinty, her mouth tightened into a straight line, and her eyebrows frowned. "We are going into the eighth grade, Delia!"

"Oh, right," I answered. As if that explained it all.

"I've got all sorts of makeup from Mom," said Mae. "Now come over here and let me see what I can do."

"What's wrong with my face?" I asked, turning toward the mirror for a closer look.

Mae took my arm and guided me to the edge of the bed. "Nothing's *wrong* with it, but it could definitely be better. Now let me do my magic."

There must have been hundreds of Avon samples—tiny eyeshadows, blushers, and lipsticks—scattered across Mae's dresser. When we were little, we used to smear that lipstick all over, and then Mae's mom would pull out her high heels and let us clomp around the house pretending we were grown up. We'd imagine we were famous, performing in front of cheering crowds. There we'd be, living room fans blowing our hair back, too-bright lipstick, singing into long wooden spoons. Sometimes the dogs downstairs would start howling as we sang. We always took that as a compliment.

I sat there as Mae worked on me.

"First, you need a good base of foundation." She dabbed a cool liquid on my face and with gentle circles rubbed it into my skin. I didn't tell Mae, but it sort of felt like I was at the Glamour Girls Nail Salon, which was right next door to Carmine's. At least that's what I imagined it would feel like.

Mae directed me as she worked. *Close your eyes. Look down. Open your mouth.*

She stood back and gave me a long stare. "Am I done?" I asked.

Mae nodded, the grin on her face about as wide as that dresser. "You look beautiful."

I'm not sure what I was expecting to see when I looked into that mirror. The first thing I noticed was my same old dull curls. There wasn't much I could do about those. I turned my face right and left, wondering where my cheekbones had come from. After that, though, what I kept staring at was my eyes. Mae had shaded my eyelids in pink and purple, then lined them underneath with black. My lashes were black, too, long and thick. I kept blinking, knowing it was me but not quite recognizing myself. For some reason, that made me think of Old Red. Maybe that was what he felt like sometimes, too.

"Now it's my turn," said Mae. She plopped down at the edge of the bed and tilted her face up. "I set a guide on the dresser. Mom gives those out to all the ladies in town who need a little help in the beauty department."

"Are you sure you want me to do it?" I wasn't exactly the person other girls turned to for beauty advice.

"You'll be fine. Just follow the instructions," said Mae. And with that she closed her eyes and waited for me to get to work.

I'll say this for how Mae looked when I was done—she sure didn't look the same as when I started. I'd tried to use the eyeshadow the way that guide said to, but the tiny plastic wand got away from me a bit. Mae's mouth gaped as she stared at her reflection, like a big river bass with ruby red lips.

"You need more practice," said Mae. Her voice didn't even sound mad. I think she took pity on me and my poor makeup skills.

It was almost dinnertime when I got home. Mama's purse was on the couch. The mail had been tossed on the coffee table. When I stopped and listened, I could hear Mama upstairs, humming a tune.

I ran up the steps and plopped myself on her bed, stretching my legs out on the comforter, my skin drinking in the cool. By the sound of it, Mama was in the bathroom, getting ready for something. There was the whir of the hair dryer, then the light click of plastic makeup cases being set on the counter. Mama didn't usually wear much makeup either.

When she came out and saw me lying there, she jumped about three feet and clutched her chest. I gave her a whistle.

"Delia!" Pink flushed her cheeks. It was the same color as Old Red's lilies. The stargazers. Directly inside the white edging, those petals shifted from light to dark and were freckled in deep red.

"What are you all dressed up for?" I asked.

Mama ran her hand over her skirt, smoothing it against her hips. "I'm going out to dinner with Mr. Pete." Her eyes caught mine. "I hope you don't mind. He called, and I knew you'd be fine on your own. But I can always reschedule."

I grinned. "I'll be fine. I am the best macaroni-and-cheese cook in all of Tucker's Ferry, if you didn't know."

When the doorbell rang, I ran to get it, greeting Mr. Pete and bringing him inside. He smelled as if he'd been rolling in pine needles, all fresh and woodsy. I'd never thought about grownups getting nervous, but he looked like Mae before a geometry test, wringing his hands and catching his bottom lip between his teeth.

When Mama came down the stairs, his breath caught in his throat. I'd never seen Mama go on a date. I half felt like I should introduce them, but of course they already knew each other.

"I'd like you both back by ten," I said, sounding as much like a schoolteacher as I could.

In that instant, I felt the thickness in the air lift. Suddenly it was Mama and Mr. Pete again, the same as they'd always been. They laughed and grinned at each other, and then Mr. Pete took Mama's hand and they walked out the door.

"You look lovely," I heard him say as they walked down the porch steps.

I was on the phone with Mae about one second after they drove away.

"You're never going to believe it," I said.

"Tommy kissed you," said Mae.

I held the phone away from my head and gave it the stink eye. "You're so cold you're at the North Pole," I yelled.

"I give up." Mae wasn't long for guessing games.

"Mama and Mr. Pete went out on a date tonight."

"No way!" Mae squealed.

I heard Mae's mom in the background. "What is it?"

From the muffled sound of Mae's reply, I could picture her standing there with one hand covering the phone. "Mrs. Burns went out with Mr. Pete tonight."

We went on like that for almost an hour, me and Mae trying to figure out what Mama and Mr. Pete were doing. We ruled out CJ's Diner. A diner simply wasn't the place to take someone on a first date. I'd never been on a real date, but even I knew that.

I thought about inviting Tommy over that night, but Mae's talk of kissing made me change my plan. The idea of kissing Tommy wasn't *so* terrible. It had crossed my mind a time or two. Once, in Old Red's garden, we were talking and standing so close that I couldn't help but notice his lips. It made my stomach tilt like I was on a ride at the fair. The kind where I got off feeling sort of woozy, but all I wanted to do was to run back around and get in line so I could go all over again.

September

That first date must have gone well, because by the time September rolled around, Mr. Pete was coming over for dinner at least once a week. In all the years I'd known him from the hardware store, I had never realized how funny he was.

Mama had turned humming into a regular hobby, and there was just the right amount of rain and sun that month so that my flowers were still blooming. They could have been featured in a magazine. I spotted B & C Gardening's flowers all over Tucker's Ferry, in the yards of everyone I'd sold seeds to. No matter where I went, there were bright splashes of me and Old Red. Sometimes when I turned a corner and saw flowers I knew were ours, I swore they were gossiping. If they told stories about me, I hoped they were good ones.

"What did we forget?" asked Mama.

We were setting the picnic tables out back, getting ready for a barbecue. Mr. Pete was turning burgers and hot dogs on the grill. There is something about the sizzle of fat over hot coals that makes my mouth water. I snuck a deviled egg, popping the whole thing in at once.

Miss Martha came with a fresh-made cole slaw. The Parkers showed up bearing pie. The crusts were golden brown, and berry juice had seeped out over the holes in the top, coating the edges with a thick, dark syrup. I might have cut a slice right then except that Mrs. Parker took those pies directly inside so the flies wouldn't feast on them.

Tommy and I sat next to each other on one of the benches. We sat so close our elbows bumped as we tried to eat. I didn't mind.

"You doing anything tomorrow?" asked Tommy.

Suddenly there were a dozen hummingbirds fluttering in my stomach. "We're going to see Old Red," I answered.

Miss Martha picked right up on that. "I need to get over there this week too. The other day I was hanging towels on the line, and I recalled the time he and Rosalea and I went out to visit his Uncle Glenn."

"I'm afraid to ask what happened," said Mrs. Parker.

"Well, Uncle Glenn brewed moonshine," said Miss Martha. "Had an illegal still in his barn. We took a notion one day that we were going to have us a taste."

"I bet this doesn't end well," said Mr. Pete. He prodded Mr. Parker with his elbow and grinned.

I ran inside and grabbed my journal, pulled the cap off my pen while I ran back outside, and wrote down the important parts as Miss Martha talked.

"That stuff burned like turpentine running down our throats," she said. "We tried to act like we were enjoying it, even though we were coughing and gagging."

"Did you get caught?" asked Tommy.

Miss Martha shook her head. "Not right then. At some point, maybe after our third glass, we realized that Uncle Glenn marked his jug. Every time he got himself a little nip, he'd take a thin grease pencil and draw a line level with the top of that clear liquid."

Mr. Pete put an arm around Mama. She rested against him. I turned and smiled at Tommy. I think that smile caught him by surprise. He put his hand over mine and squeezed.

"So how did you replace that missing moonshine?" I asked.

"I'd have drawn another line," said Mr. Parker. He said it matter-of-factly, as if he'd done it a million times, which was impossible to imagine. Mr. Parker was straighter than a ruler.

Mrs. Parker cocked her head and gave him a look that said she didn't quite believe him either. "You're such a rebel, dear."

Tommy and I laughed, then waited for Miss Martha to go on.

"Never thought of finding that grease pencil. Instead, we added water to that white lightning until it reached his line."

"Oh no," said Mr. Pete. "You ruined it."

Miss Martha nodded. "That's what Uncle Glenn thought, too, after he slipped out to the barn for his next nip." She slapped her thigh, thinking about it. "Old Red said he bet folks from Wayne to Kanawha County heard Uncle Glenn scream."

"What happened to all of you?" asked Tommy.

"Old Red never told who was with him, so we got away scot-free. Poor Redford, on the other hand, had to shovel manure from Uncle Glenn's barn for two months."

I could see the flowers bending toward us, taking in every word. The fireflies were dancing too, lighting up and twirling around, as if our stories had taken flight. I watched them go, carrying bits of our tales off into the dusk.

Those stories were still spinning in my mind when we pulled up to Riverdale the next day. Chrysanthemums in gold and russet lined the sidewalk. I led the way past the front desk and down the hall to Old Red's room.

"I'll see you both in a few minutes," said Mama. She turned down another hall, heading to the cafeteria so she could get us something to drink.

Old Red was watching television when I came in, sitting on the couch. I reached down and gave him a hug. "Brought some more memories," I said, waving the pages in my hand. "Miss Martha told us all about the moonshine." I tried to look disapproving but ended up giggling instead. Up onto the wall went my new stories and photographs. In another few months that wall would be filled with tales, I was certain.

Old Red came over to his remembering wall and together we read stories.

"Why didn't you tell on Miss Martha and Rosalea?" I asked. "When you got caught with the moonshine."

Mr. Clancy skimmed the paper, reading through the words I wrote. Then he pressed both hands onto his cane. "Because they didn't deserve it."

I thought about that.

When I got in trouble I wanted Mae or Tommy—or anyone, really—to get in trouble too, so I wouldn't be alone in my suffering. But maybe suffering is one of those things that can't really be shared.

When Mama came into the room carrying our sodas, she reminded me of someone I'd seen in a photo. Her hair, let out of its ponytail, hung long and loose at her neck, and she had pulled on the sweater she'd brought. The air conditioning was on full blast at Riverdale.

I heard Old Red gasp, his eyes fixed on Mama. Then he turned and started across that room. He moved slowly, leaning heavy on that cane. I watched as he reached out a hand and took hers. Mama didn't say a word.

"You've come back to me," said Old Red. Then he wrapped Mama in a hug.

Come back. The words echoed in my head, but I had no idea what they meant.

I sat there for a minute, trying to figure out what was happening. I'd never seen Old Red give Mama a hug except at church, when everyone was shaking hands and greeting one another during the visiting part of the service. The skin on my arms tingled. Something wasn't right.

Then one of those photographs on the wall caught my attention. I squinted at it, then looked at Mama. My breath quickened.

With her face tilted and that blond hair falling across her eyes, I knew exactly who Old Red thought she was. Mama looked like Rosalea.

There was a brightness in his eyes as he held Mama's face. He cupped her chin like she was a porcelain doll. Then he ran a hand over her hair.

"You are so beautiful," said Old Red. "I've missed you."

For a second I wondered what Mama would say. I prayed she wouldn't correct him, tell him that it was all a mistake. I'd heard Miss Martha say that correcting him wasn't a good idea. More than anything in my life, at that moment, all I wanted was for Old Red to have a few more minutes with Rosalea.

"I've missed you too," said Mama. Her smile was soft.

My heart felt swollen against my ribs. My chin quivered. I let out a long, slow breath I hadn't even realized I was holding.

Then Old Red reached out to Mama. "Dance with me," he whispered.

Mama nodded. They wrapped their arms around one another and started swaying side to side. Old Red usually struggled without that cane, but at that moment, with Rosalea in his arms, his steps were sure and steady.

I went over to the radio and fiddled with the tuner until I found the right station. It was the kind Old Red had on sometimes at his house. When I turned up the volume, the room was filled with music. As they danced, I could almost see that tune swirling and dancing right alongside.

Mama laid her head on Old Red's shoulder. He looked stronger somehow. It was as if the years had melted away and Old Red had become young again. I could see the boy who had squeezed through the bus door, the young man who had stood in the road reciting poetry. I could see the groom at Rosalea's wedding and the dad who'd tossed a baseball in the backyard with Eddie. Each of those stories was taped to the wall.

As Mama and Old Red turned, making their way across that floor, I held completely still, afraid of doing anything that might ruin the moment. Both of them had their eyes closed; their faces almost glowed. Now and then Old Red stopped. He'd stare at Mama, seeing only Rosalea, and kiss her cheek, making sure she was there.

He stared at her the way folks stare at a rainbow, taking in all that unexpected beauty, not wanting to look away in case it might disappear.

October

I didn't notice the For Sale sign at first. I was busy cutting and clipping, collecting seeds and giving those flowers an update. In quiet words, I told them about Old Red mistaking Mama for Rosalea. While I talked, I caught myself smiling. It didn't seem right to be sad for Old Red when dancing with Rosalea had made him so happy. The flowers listened, petals facing me, silent. Maybe it was the wind, but as they swayed, it felt like they were encouraging me to go on.

Old Red was changing. It was happening faster than I expected. My hands shook even as I thought about it. Taking a deep breath, I walked to the edge of the fence and started in with the rake.

The seasons were starting to change, too. There was a cool breeze in the air. The leaves were falling, the gardens all over Tucker's Ferry were shriveling up, and wherever I went, folks were bundled in thick sweaters and fall jackets.

As I pulled that rake, the sign caught my attention. I'm not sure how I missed it when I came through the gate. The metal stakes were shoved into the ground directly in front of the fence near the patch of zinnias. Printed at the top, in bold block letters, was WALKER REALTY. *For more information*, it said at the bottom, *call Grady Walker*. Then it listed his number. Grady owned the only realty company in town. He sold almost every house in Tucker's Ferry.

Reaching over the fence, I grabbed that sign with one

hand and gave it a shake. Then I dropped my rake and walked around the fence so I could get a better grip. At first I tugged. Then I pulled. Then I started beating on it like it was my worst enemy, swinging that rake into the side and kicking with all my might. That metal sign cried out after each hit. Or maybe that was me. Either way, it was a terrible noise.

When the sign lay on the lawn, I felt empty. My breathing was heavy, coming in short, hard spurts. I slumped to the ground, my back against the fence.

Everything at Old Red's house felt different now. The front door was locked tight. And Rex had gone home with Eddie. I missed that mangy old mutt being sprawled out on the front porch, one paw dangling over the top step, growling a hello. Old Red wasn't tapping his cane and shouting a greeting at each passerby. Even the bees were quieter. It was as if they'd taken a cue from the butterflies and hummingbirds and were trying to slip in and out without making a sound.

If the house was for sale, this would be my last year in the garden. Thinking about Old Red being gone made me feel empty inside. I walked up the steps and ran my hand over the wooden porch swing. The seat was smooth and indented, rubbed away by years of sitting. Even the hardest things can be worn down. Bit by bit, breath by breath.

I stared out at the garden. If flowers could remember, the ones belonging to Old Red were full of stories. I'd gather seeds one more time, fill my jars with history. Then it would be up to me to keep all those memories alive.

After storing my tools and closing up the garage, I walked to the post office. If anyone knew more about Old Red's house going up for sale, it was Miss Martha. Grady must have been in, and as sure as the sun rises, Miss Martha was bound to have heard all about it.

When I came through the door, there were two people in line waiting to mail packages. The room felt full, the air almost bubbling with chitchat and laughter. I stood by the corkboard that was covered with announcements and want ads and waited for Miss Martha to finish. A few of the announcements were months out of date. I unpinned those and tossed them in the trash, then lined up the tacks so they'd be easy to find.

"Delia!" cried Miss Martha when she spied me.

I didn't return her smile. "There's a For Sale sign up at Mr. Clancy's," I said.

Miss Martha's face went slack, as if all the emotion had been washed away. "Grady told me that was coming."

"If Eddie's selling the house," I said, "that means he doesn't think Old Red will be coming home."

The words lingered there, hanging over our heads, as if they had no place better to go.

By the next morning, the world had taken on my mood. It was overcast, the sky threatening rain. I went to church with Mama. My heart was still bound and tied. When we passed Mr. Clancy's house, the For Sale sign was propped squarely in the front yard. Grady had come back and fixed it. Mama had made me call him and confess.

Inside the church it was dark as gray felt. The stained-glass windows, usually bright and cheerful with rays of sun streaming through, stared down at me with cold, flat eyes. We took our seats and I opened up the program.

Turned out that Sunday was a special day at the First Congregational Church of Christ. With all that was happening, I'd forgotten about the laying on of hands. We only did it a few times a year. On those days Preacher Jenkins worked himself into a lather as he preached, hoping to convert more souls to the Lord.

I sat up a little straighter as the organ started to play.

When the choir began singing at the back of the church I turned around to look. The choir members were bunched up by the double doors, their voices pouring down the aisle. Someone had a tambourine and was keeping time. Those small metal jingles were bright and bouncy, and so was the choir as they made their way up front. I couldn't help but watch as all those swaying black robes strolled past, each step landing exactly on the beat.

I'd never once gone up front during the laying on of hands. It was all I could think about as Preacher Jenkins spoke. His words went in one ear and right out the other. Even though I stared in his general direction as he preached, my mind was busy working up the courage to walk up that aisle.

When the sermon was over, the preacher wiped the sweat from his face and stood directly up front. He cued the organist, who began to play. The song was low and deep, the kind of tune that made folks bow their heads and stare at their laps.

He didn't say anything for a little while, just let the music settle over us like a fog, until the whole room was calm. When he finally spoke, his voice didn't thunder across that sanctuary; instead, it matched that music, soft and gentle. Although his big voice was powerful, I think that soft voice made us pay even more attention. I could see folks tilting their ears toward the front, making sure they caught every word.

"We've had a special guest today," said Preacher Jenkins in that quiet voice.

I glanced around, but all I saw were our regular friends and neighbors. There weren't any unfamiliar faces. I figured whoever it was must be sitting in the back.

"A special guest that comes every Sunday, rain or shine." The preacher held up his Bible. "We don't need a fancy church for Him to come. Or a choir. Or even a preacher." His voice trailed off at the end. "What we need is you."

Preacher Jenkins gestured then, motioning the elders to come forward. They stood in two small groups, one on the left side of the aisle and the other on the right.

"In the Good Book it tells us that if we gather in His name, then He is here also," said Preacher Jenkins. He glanced around the church and held his hands out as if he might hug us all. "Come and find the Lord."

A few folks walked straight down the aisle, then veered left or right once they reached the end. I kept my eyes low, but I watched, paying close attention to how the whole thing worked. The church elders listened as the person who had come forward spoke. I couldn't hear a thing, but I guessed that the person was talking about a problem in their life. The elders took in every word, nodding, their faces serious. Then they placed their hands on that person, touching an arm or shoulder, and they all bowed their heads to pray.

I admired those people who could walk down the aisle and let the entire town know that something in their life was wrong. Before the lightning, Mama and I tried to pretend that things were perfect, that we had it all worked out. But as it turned out, it was better when people knew, because then folks were able to help.

When there was no one up with the elders and no one

waiting in the aisle, I took a deep breath and stood. Then I stepped out of that pew and walked straight to the front of the church. One of the elders on the right side gave me a nod, so I went there. The three huddled around me when I arrived, almost enclosing me. In that second I felt separated from the rest of the church, as if I was in a completely different place and time.

"What is laying heavy on your mind, my dear?" one of the elders asked.

"It's Old Red," I answered, my voice barely a whisper. "I'd like to pray for Mr. Clancy."

"Okay," said another elder. "Is there anything in particular you'd like to ask for?"

I swallowed hard before I answered. "I'd like to pray that God would take some of my memory and give it to Old Red."

They were silent for a moment. I thought maybe I'd asked for the wrong thing, messed up my praying one more time.

"All right, then," said the third elder. "Let us pray."

They had their arms draped around my back and holding on to my arms so that even if I fainted they'd keep me standing upright. I could feel the warmth of their skin through my dress.

As they prayed, I closed my eyes, letting myself go to the power of their words. I forgot about the rest of Tucker's Ferry sitting behind me in those pews. That prayer spun round and round and I imagined the rug Mr. Clancy had shown me filling up.

There was something different about that prayer. Maybe Preacher Jenkins was right and we did have a special guest that day. And maybe that special guest had come and listened in on my prayer, too. I'm not sure how else I can explain what happened next. Because when those elders were saying *Amen*, a strong perfume washed over me in that church. I breathed deep. Although I'd never smelled it before, I knew exactly what it was. It was the scent of pansies.

November

The night before I went to see Old Red I had a dream. In it I was gardening. It was the planting season, the earth warm and ready for life. I'd grown thousands of seedlings in tiny plastic pots. They went on forever across the front porch and onto the yard.

Then I took those thousands of seedlings, which could never have fit in my wagon in real life, and started off down the road. I hadn't gone very far before I noticed a bare speck of dirt calling out to me. It was a lonely patch of earth, a few scraggly bits of grass and some dusty soil. There is nothing that wouldn't have improved that little spot. Even a tossed-away bottle cap would have proved that someone had passed by, had at least noticed that corner of Tucker's Ferry.

I think time moves faster in dreams than in real life, because without giving it much thought I pulled out my spade, popped a seedling from its pack, and tucked it in the ground. Then I let the watering can rain down until the ground had taken a long, cool drink. The seedling was bent over, one of its leaves almost touching the dirt, as if it was trying to shake hands and introduce itself.

Suddenly I started spying bare spots everywhere I looked. Little specks of dirt were raising their hands all over the place. *Me! Me!* they said. So there I went, watching and listening for the cries of the forgotten patches and then marching over and filling them up.

By the time I woke up, I'd planted all of those seedlings, and my watering can had somehow never run dry. I'd criss-crossed Tucker's Ferry planting flowers into nooks and crannies no one else had noticed. I ran to the window and looked out front, just to make sure it wasn't spring. The dream had felt so real.

As I rode to Riverdale, I thought about those flowers. There wasn't a doubt in my mind that Old Red would love the idea of sneaking down side roads searching for places that needed a bit more color and love. We would paint the town.

When I got to Mr. Clancy's room, it was empty. That happened sometimes when Old Red had doctor's appointments. He had doctors that checked his memory and kept tabs on his heart, which wasn't doing very well either. I'd heard Mama's whispered phone calls with Miss Martha.

As always, I went straight to the wall of memories. It had become the talk of Riverdale. I'd seen nurses and other patients and even their families in here reading the stories and getting close to the photographs. They'd squint their eyes and stare at the pictures, trying to figure out from the stories who was who.

In five months, that wall had been completely covered in Old Red. There were stories from his youngest days all the way up to us deciding to start a flower business. I'd made a big poster board that read *B & C Gardening* and had Mama snap a photo of us to put on it. When I started gathering memories, I never could have predicted it would turn out that perfect. It was a life-size autobiography.

When the nurse wheeled Old Red in, I was watching television. Football was on, which wasn't my favorite, but there wasn't much to choose from on Saturday afternoon. It was either that, a fancy commercial for frying pans, or an old kung fu movie.

"Hey there, Mr. Clancy," I said. "I brought some cookies with me." I pointed to a small table near the television. "Mama baked them last night."

The nurse with him was one I hadn't met before. Her eyes lit up when she saw those chocolate chips. "Isn't that nice! Mind if I have one?"

"Go ahead," I answered. "Help yourself."

Old Red sat down on the couch. That was where he spent most of his time now, just sitting. Walking had become a tricky proposition. In the last few months his legs had gone all rubbery, as if even they were forgetting how they worked.

I set two cookies on a paper plate in front of him. "Here you go," I said. "Your favorite."

He gave me a smile. "Thank you kindly, my dear."

Old Red never called me *my dear*. My ears picked that up right away. I glanced at him, but he was staring at those cookies, trying to figure out which one to eat first.

"I'll let you two visit," said the nurse. "I've got to get back to work anyway." She held up the last bite of chocolate chip. "Thanks so much for the treat."

Mr. Clancy barely turned her way as she left. Didn't say goodbye or anything. That struck me as odd, too.

I ran out to the hall, catching the nurse before she'd gotten too far. "Excuse me," I said. "I didn't want to ask in front of Old Red, but is he okay?" I tucked my curls behind my ears.

The nurse touched my hand, connecting us. "Some days are better, some are worse. Today is a worse day."

I could feel my entire face turn down at the edges.

"Are you his granddaughter?" she asked.

Without even thinking, I nodded. "And we sell flowers together. Old Red is the best gardener in all of Tucker's Ferry." For some reason it was important to me that she know that. In that moment I wanted her to know who he was before he started getting erased. My words poured out fast. "He was a war hero, too, and a poet, and when he was young he was the West Virginia state champion in the mile."

"He's lucky to have someone like you to love him." She gave my hand a squeeze. "How about you get back in there? Never know—maybe today will turn into a good day, now that you're here."

I stared at the linoleum as I walked, taking small steps. Almost not wanting to get there. More than half afraid of what I might find.

Old Red was sound asleep on that couch when I turned in to the room. His head lay straight back on the cushions. There was still one cookie on the plate in front of him. I clicked the television off and grabbed my backpack. I had some loose-leaf paper and a pen, just what I needed to record some of my own memories for the wall.

I wrote about me stealing flowers from his garden, and the time at the creek when I'd sung church-school songs and he told me I sounded just like Rosalea. Guess she and I were tied for having the worst singing voice in Tucker's Ferry. I remembered laughing so hard my stomach hurt. Then I wrote about him helping with my broken-down house and teaching me all the secrets of the garden.

While I was taping them up amid all the other tales,

I heard Old Red stir. I sat down in the chair next to him and watched as he woke up. Then I patted him on the hand. "Morning, sleeping beauty," I said. That was something Mama said to me sometimes, especially on days when I slept later than usual. Even though it was the late afternoon, I figured it still fit.

"I'm thirsty," he said.

I fetched a plastic cup from the counter and poured some water from the tap.

"Mr. Clancy, I had the best dream last night," I told him. "I imagined that I ran all over Tucker's Ferry planting flowers from the seeds in your garden. There wasn't a single bare patch that I didn't cover." I sighed, picturing summer. "Close your eyes. Can't you see it? Can't you see the entire town blooming?"

My voice was almost bursting as I spoke. I thought Old Red would be bursting too, but he was fiddling with the remote control, trying to turn the television back on.

"Here," I said, taking it from him. "The 'on' button is at the top. See?"

"Okay," he said. The word was flat.

That was when the room started getting smaller. Squeezing me until I could barely breathe. The nurse was right. It was a bad day.

"Mr. Clancy," I whispered, "do you know who I am?"

When he spoke, his voice was matter-of-fact, as if I was no different from one of the nurses. "You're the girl who comes sometimes. The one who hangs things on the wall." Then he paused. "You seem awful nice."

I felt my mouth turn under and my chin start to quiver.

My eyes started blinking faster than normal and my chest tightened. I caught my tongue between my teeth and pressed down hard.

Old Red set his hand on top of mine and smiled. "You sound familiar, though, like a young girl I used to know."

I nodded, and then I whispered, "I bet her name was Delia."

December

Even though Mama and Miss Martha had tried to prepare me for the day when Old Red would forget me, I never really thought it would happen. I thought maybe I was buried deep enough in his heart to make forgetting impossible. I was wrong.

Mama hugged me close that night when I came home from Riverdale. I couldn't even speak; the words got tangled up in my throat. But Mama looked into my eyes, and she knew.

"Oh no," was all she said. And then she wrapped her arms around me and held on tight.

My tears came from a deep well. Mama kept stroking my hair, half rocking me the way a mother might rock a baby when they're falling asleep.

When my breathing was regular again, I told her what had happened.

"He said I sounded like someone he knew." Just saying it aloud made me start weeping all over again. My whole body sagged into Mama.

I think God must have known how I was feeling, because December suddenly turned colder than usual. It was a wet cold, the type that burrowed through my coat, stabbing me with icy points. No matter what I did, it seemed I couldn't keep warm.

At night, curled into a tight ball on my bed, I replayed Mr. Clancy's words over and over. I could see the blank expression on his face as he looked at me. But thinking about it didn't change the ending.

Mae tried to drag me out of my funk. "Come on," she said one Saturday afternoon. "You and I are going to the movies."

Seeing as Mae's mom was waiting for us in the driveway, there wasn't much I could say but yes. The theater near the mall, maybe fifteen minutes down the road, played eight movies. Mae had her mind set on one about a group of girls who went to a dude ranch for their summer vacation.

"It's going to be hilarious," she said. "The girls are from the city and don't know the first thing about bringing in a herd."

I gave Mae an eyebrow, knowing for a fact that beyond a few riding lessons when she was in elementary school, Mae wasn't exactly an expert in that either. But she rattled off bits of the story she'd heard from other kids. "And there's a part where they need to lasso a calf and one of the girls ends up almost hog-tying her friend. Sarah said that about made her pee her pants."

My mood lifted a little as I grinned.

"Some popcorn?" said Mae. She held out the extra-large tub she'd ordered. At the movies, Mae and I shared everything.

The popcorn bucket was about as big as a bushel basket and was heaped in a mound at the top. The smell of melted butter and salt floated over us. We both dug in as we got to our seats. Fresh popcorn is near impossible to resist, second only to fresh doughnuts.

"If ever there was a girl who needed to laugh," said Mae, "I think you're her."

When the lights went dim and the screen lit up, Mae balanced the tub of popcorn on top of both of our knees. The kids at school were right—that movie made me laugh until I was gasping for breath and holding my aching sides. Of course, my aching sides might also have been from the popcorn. Mae and I finished the entire tub.

"One more week till Christmas break," I said as we walked out of the theater.

"Thank the Lord," answered Mae.

Tucker's Ferry was decorated in her holiday finery. There were fake evergreen wreaths hanging from the lampposts and holiday flags hanging from storefronts, and the IGA had a wide red ribbon wrapped around the roof, with a bow the size of a car smack dab on top. The Perkins family owned the IGA and did that every year. Christmas was their favorite holiday.

In the center of town was the municipal park. As soon as the wishbone from the Thanksgiving turkey had been broken in two, park officials began decorating our small square. I bet if someone measured lightbulbs per square inch, we might have set a record. In front were blinking Santas and reindeer that moved their heads up and down. There were red and green dancing elves and enough candy canes to scare any dentist into early retirement. A gazebo in the center of the park had white twinkly lights hanging from the roof. They almost looked like icicles.

Tucker's Ferry was a popular place in December with people driving in to see the lights and shop at the stores, which all stayed open late and served up free hot cider and cookies. A person could walk from store to store and eat enough for dinner. That was why Tommy wanted to go when he stopped over at my house later that night.

"Come on, Delia. It'll be fun," he said.

Mama gave me a nod. "Get out for a little while. The fresh air will do you good."

I went upstairs and pulled on a sweater. When I came back down, Tommy had already pulled out my coat and hat and mittens. I grinned, remembering how annoying I used to think Tommy was. But I liked how he held open doors and always let me go first. That part never felt annoying.

We held hands as we walked, his fingers squeezing mine through all that wool.

"Have you seen Old Red lately?" I asked Tommy. I hadn't gone back since the forgetting. And I wasn't sure if I could go back again.

Tommy nodded. "He doesn't remember any of us. It's like he's getting younger in that place. Mom put his shoes on him the other day and tied them. We watched some football together, but I'm not even sure he understood the score."

I know it was wrong, but part of me was glad Mr. Clancy couldn't remember the Parkers either.

As we rounded the corner to town, I spotted that winning fire hydrant. The one that had been painted like a Continental soldier. Some clever person had knitted that soldier a hat. It even had a red, white, and blue pom-pom on top.

"Look at that," I said, pointing.

"He looks ready to go sledding," said Tommy.

I gave him a gentle shove. "Except for the rifle."

That made us both laugh.

We walked through town, moving in time to the holiday

music that was being piped from a loudspeaker at the park. It was easy to stay warm walking in and out of shops, our mittens almost always wrapped around a steaming cup of cider.

I bought a magnet from Miss Carmine. It said, *When I grow up, I want to be a dog.* It made me think of Rex lolling about on the porch, that big old tongue hanging from one side of his mouth. I hoped Rex was enjoying his new life in Ohio.

"You know," I said to Tommy, "I never thought I'd miss Rex. That dog tried to eat us for years."

"He came close a few times," said Tommy.

We were still smiling when we saw the park. The lights danced and blinked and sparkled.

Cars circled the park slow. We followed the signs that said *Start Here* and wandered our way through. It was a maze of lights. Tommy's face shone red and green and white from the reflection.

We walked past the ballerinas and nutcrackers, the snowflakes and gingerbread men, until we came to the gazebo. Tommy pulled me in after him. We rested against the railing and gazed out over the entire display. It was like we'd been swallowed by a star.

When I turned around, Tommy had a small box in his hand.

"I know it's not Christmas yet," he said. "But I wanted you to open this tonight."

I could feel my cheeks get warm. My own gift for him was sitting in my bedroom. Not yet wrapped.

Sitting on the cold wooden bench, I pulled off my mittens and tugged at the paper. Inside was a jewelry box. When I opened it, my breath caught in my throat. It was a heart, dangling on a thin silver chain.

Tommy helped me put it on, which took a while since our fingers were about half frozen. "How's it look?" I asked.

"Pretty," he answered. When he said it he was looking straight into my eyes.

I'm not sure what came over me then. Maybe it was the necklace or the lights or all that apple cider, but I threw my arms around him and hugged him tight. He hugged me too.

Our faces were close, so close I could feel his breath. I leaned forward and shut my eyes. Then I kissed Tommy Parker. Right there in that gazebo, not caring who in Tucker's Ferry might see us.

It was just a little kiss, but it took my breath away. When we pulled apart his cheeks were red. I bet mine were too, because even though it was night, I swear I could feel the sun.

When I walked through the door Mama was sitting on the couch, reading a book.

"Looks like someone had a good night," she said.

I pulled off my jacket and hat and mittens. My hand went straight to my neck. "Look what Tommy gave me." I lifted my chin so she could see the necklace.

Mama admired it. "It's lovely."

I fingered that heart all the way upstairs to my room.

Before I went to sleep, I put the necklace on my night table. With my finger I traced a line across the smooth silver. Then I picked up my journal and wrote it all down. I wrote about the movie, the lights, the gift, and the kiss, everything I saw, smelled, tasted, heard, and felt. It was definitely a memory worth keeping.

January

I was at the post office picking up our mail when I heard that Grady Walker had sold Old Red's house. As usual, there was a line of folks waiting to buy stamps and mail packages. Each one of them took their turn chatting with Miss Martha.

"I heard it this morning at CJ's Diner," said Mrs. Williams. "Grady was in there himself, eating fried eggs and bacon."

If they were talking about it at the diner, then Mama would know all about it too. I pulled the envelopes and magazines from our slot and closed the small bronze door. Taking a deep breath, I walked toward Miss Martha's window so I could hear more.

"He say anything about the folks who bought it?" asked Miss Martha.

Mrs. Williams shook her head. "Think they're from Kentucky, but I may have got that wrong. Frank had a sneezing attack right about that time. That man eats his eggs with so much pepper you'd think they were fried black. Don't know how he can taste a thing."

"Won't be the same, will it?" asked Miss Martha. "Without Old Red out there on that porch next summer, greeting us all every time we pass by."

"We'll have to let the new family know they've got big shoes to fill," said Mrs. Williams.

"Kentucky," I whispered as I slipped out the door. I

started for home, but on the way my eyes scanned the distance, searching out that sign even before I had turned onto Old Red's street.

Sure enough, crossing out the words *For Sale* like one of those beauty-pageant sashes were those four little letters, *S-O-L-D*. I pushed through the gate, walked up to the porch, and sat down on the swing. Without even trying, I thought back to all the times Old Red and I had sat there together. Those tarnished metal chains had never given up, despite all their complaining. I pushed off to get it moving, then tucked my legs up under me, partly to stay warm and partly to make myself believe that Mr. Clancy was sitting next to me, keeping us going with his cane.

When the swing stopped I didn't move. I stared at the front yard. The flowers seemed like dead twigs now, all their strength and beauty hidden from view. Kind of like Old Red.

The new people probably had no idea what they were getting. Even if Grady had told them about the flowers, I'm sure they couldn't imagine it half as good as it really was. I closed my eyes and said a little prayer that the new folks from Kentucky liked to garden.

I shut the gate behind me and gave that house one long last look. Even though I knew I'd see it every day, something about that Sold sign made this time feel like goodbye. The house had an empty look about it, the same way my house had looked after the lightning. Whatever spirit once lived there had up and flown away.

Mama told Old Red all about the news when we went to visit that night. He lay in bed most of the time now, drifting in and out of sleep while we were there. I washed his face with a damp cloth and combed his hair anyway. He needed to look good for the nurses, especially the one with the gardenia perfume.

While Mama talked I held on to Old Red's hand, gently rubbing my skin over his. I wanted to feel connected. Somewhere deep down, I hoped he knew it was me.

"Mr. Clancy," Mama said, "there's going to be a new family living in your house."

"They have kids?" I asked.

Mama nodded. "Grady says they do. Three of them. Two girls and a boy. Youngest is five and the oldest nine."

"They like gardening?" I gave Mama a raised eyebrow.

The grin that crossed Mama's face lit up the entire room. "I hear the wife was beside herself when she learned that the entire front yard is planted with heirloom flowers."

I patted Mr. Clancy on the shoulder. "Hear that? I'll stop by as soon as they move in. I'll make sure they take good care of it."

Mama stood up and went to the wall. I could see her reading the stories one after another. When she turned, her face was a mix of wonder and awe, the way I'd seen grownups look when they were staring at babies.

"This is amazing, you know. All these stories." She motioned for me to join her. "I bet each visitor has read something."

I set Old Red's hand back on the blanket and walked to her side. "I thought I could keep him from forgetting." My eyes clung to the floor.

With a gentle hand Mama lifted my chin until she could see directly into my face. "You should be so proud. Every single person, and I mean all the doctors and nurses as well as all his friends from Tucker's Ferry, they all got to meet Old Red." Her voice shook.

"The *real* Old Red," I said, swallowing hard.

"Exactly," said Mama. She rested her cheek against my hair. "The brave, strong, kind, and adventurous man that he was."

With both hands she pushed on my shoulders until we were an arm's length apart. "You know, you're just like him."

It was the nicest compliment Mama had ever given me.

We each kissed Old Red on the forehead before we left. As I ran my hand over the soft stubble on his cheek, he opened his eyes. I gave him a smile.

"Hi there, Mr. Clancy."

"Hi," he said back. His gaze took in me and Mama. "Angels," he whispered. Then his eyelids began to close again, as if his dream was pulling him back to sleep.

Mama and I told Mrs. Parker that story the following week. We were there for dinner, us and Mr. Pete. It was a football playoff day, and the Parkers had invited us over for all the fun. The boys were in the living room screaming at the television, big bowls of chips lined up in front of them. Every now and then we'd hear them yell, and Mrs. Parker and Mama and I would just shake our heads.

Of course telling that story put a kink in our plans. As Mama spoke, Mrs. Parker sobbed. I doled out tissues until her nose stopped running; then I pulled my chair next to hers and rubbed her back. The same way she'd done for me after Mama's accident.

"Look at me," said Mrs. Parker. "I've got dinner to cook and I'm a complete wreck."

"We won't starve to death," I said.

Mama nodded. "Even if the boys think they will."

That made all three of us grin.

After a few more tissues, Mrs. Parker stood and gave me a hug. She hugged Mama too. Then we got back to cooking.

"Delia," said Mrs. Parker, "would you mind doing me a favor?"

"Sure," I answered.

"See that bowl of candy canes over there?" She pointed to the corner of the counter. "Could you crush those for me?"

Mrs. Parker had a recipe for peppermint ice cream, and she always waited until January to make it so she could use up her leftover holiday candy. It was sort of like eating frozen toothpaste, except much better.

I opened the plastic on those two-inch canes and dumped them into a brown paper bag. Then I carried it with me out to the garage. I needed a rubber mallet so I could beat those candy canes into smithereens.

"Need some help?" said a voice behind me just as I was getting ready to clobber that bag.

It was Tommy. "Not really," I said, smiling at him. "But I'll let you help anyway."

I took the first swing. Those candy canes didn't stand a chance.

It felt good to hold that mallet. Reminded me of my gardening shears. I was itching for spring. The flowers were still asleep, but they'd wake up as soon as the ground began to warm. And I'd be ready. I had promised Old Red that it was going to be a bang-up year for B & C Gardening.

"Wait," I said, holding my arm out and stopping Tommy

midway up the front steps. "Hear that?" I tilted my ear toward the woods.

"Hear what?" asked Tommy.

"Shhh," I said. "There it is again. It sounds like a whip-poorwill." I glanced at Tommy. "But it can't be. They fly south in the winter." I remembered what the Thread-Bears had told me, about those birds catching souls.

When we walked back through the front door, I knew something was wrong. The television had been turned off, and all the grownups, the Parkers, Mama, and Mr. Pete, were sitting together, their heads hanging low.

I clutched onto that brown bag like it was a life jacket. Tommy stood directly behind me, so close I could feel his chest behind my back. I leaned back just a little.

"What is it?" I asked. "What happened?"

In the silence I could hear the clock ticking.

Mama came to me and gently took the paper bag. Then she held my hands. "Eddie just called."

Eddie had been in town for about a week. He'd arrived just a day or two after our last visit with Mr. Clancy. Miss Martha said he was staying at Riverdale. They had a place for him to sleep so he could be with his dad all the time.

I stared at the telephone, avoiding Mama's eyes. Avoiding everyone's eyes, for fear of what I'd see there. Didn't matter. I heard the words anyway.

"Old Red's heart," she said. "It just gave out."

I knew what was coming next. Even still, my breath caught in my throat when Mama said it.

"He's gone."

February

Mama bought me a new black dress for the funeral. The fabric lay heavy on my skin, squeezing my ribs and pinching at my neck. Each gulp of air hurt.

When we arrived at the church, the hearse from the funeral home was already there. Waiting. Two men in black suits stood by the back door. Their faces were somber as they watched us, their breath clouds of white in the cold. Mama and I stood together on the asphalt, shivering under our coats. Hot tears burned the corners of my eyes as I stared at that casket in the back of the car.

One by one, the folks closest to Old Red arrived. Mr. Parker brushed Tommy's lapels and straightened his tie. I'd never seen Tommy in a suit. It made him seem taller, and older. The old ladies at church had been right all along. He was handsome.

Mama hugged the Parkers, and I did too.

I laid my head on Tommy's chest. "I still can't believe it."

Tommy's eyes were as red as mine. He didn't say a word, just nodded, his lips pressed tightly together. I gave his hand a squeeze and he held on, gripping me as if he was falling and I was the only person left in the world to catch him. I didn't even think about letting go.

When enough men had arrived, the folks from the funeral home opened the back of the hearse and slid the casket out. The men who were gathered around, including Tommy, took a hold of the silver bars that lined the side. I swallowed hard as they lifted it from the car and then carried Old Red through the doors of the First Congregational Church of Christ.

Mama and I followed behind, our steps slow and measured. Going into the church meant saying goodbye, and I wasn't ready for that. I clutched Mama and she held tight to Miss Martha, who probably hurt more than all of us put together.

We stopped in the entrance and greeted Eddie, who was shaking hands and talking to each guest. I hadn't noticed it before, but he looked a lot like Old Red. They had the same blue eyes and the thick curly mop of hair that I'd seen in the pictures and heard about in the stories. I could feel my chin shake as I thought about those tales, about all the fun things Old Red would never do again.

When it was our turn, Mama signed the guest book for both of us.

"Delia," Eddie said, "before his memory faded, Dad talked about you all the time." My throat felt raw. "He was so proud that Tucker's Ferry was going to have another Rosalea when it came to gardening."

I shook my head. "I'm not nearly as good as Rosalea."

Eddie took my hand in his. "Dad thought you were even better. Said you could talk to the flowers."

I felt a tear drip down my face when he said that. My nose was running too. Somehow I managed to give him a hug and whisper *Thank you.*

"I've got a feeling we're going to need these," said Mama, taking a full box of tissues from a side table as we walked into the sanctuary. She wrapped an arm around my waist and gave me a squeeze.

They had the casket open up front. People were already standing in line down one aisle, waiting to pay their last respects. As they got to Old Red, I could see them reaching out to touch him, then kissing his forehead one last time. I clutched that box of tissues and tried to count the stained-glass windows.

Mr. Pete went first, then Mama. She ran a gentle finger down Old Red's cheek and touched the rose pinned to his lapel. I stared at his face. Waiting for him to breathe. Waiting for him to open his eyes. Except the person in that casket wasn't really Old Red.

"It doesn't even look like him," I said to Mama, my voice barely there.

The angles of his face were wrong; he was too shallow. His hair was combed in a way that he had never worn it, and his skin, which had always had a tinge of tan from being in the garden, was pale and waxy.

"I wish they had put him in his gardening clothes," I said.

Preacher Jenkins raised his arms to heaven once everyone was seated. "Brothers and sisters, welcome!" His voice was strong and sure. "Today we are here to celebrate the life of Redford Clancy."

There were a few cries of *Amen* from the congregation.

"I say *celebrate*, because we know where our Brother Clancy has gone." He placed his hands on the casket. "As sure as I'm standing here before you, Old Red is not *here*, in this place. He is *there*, in that place." The preacher raised his hands and eyes toward heaven. "He has been reborn, beckoned by his own family, extending back to the beginning of time, to come and join them."

The preacher looked everyone in the eye. "Jesus was waiting for him too."

That's right! came from the back.

Preacher Jenkins continued. "And guess who was standing right behind our Lord and Savior, arms outstretched, waiting for her Old Red? Without a doubt it was his beloved Rosalea."

I thought about how Old Red danced with Mama, holding her face like it was a fancy porcelain teacup. There were sniffles all around. I handed Miss Martha another tissue.

Preacher Jenkins signaled the choir. There were a few clear notes from the piano. "Open your spirit," he said, "to the words Old Red wanted you to hear this very day." Then they began. It was a song about kneeling at the cross. I closed my eyes and let the music wash over me.

When it was time for sharing, Eddie got up to speak. He stood there, just as he had in the entrance when he greeted us, and told his own stories. Even as I dabbed my eyes, I was laughing. And it was the laughing that made me feel like Old Red was still there.

While the voices were quieter than they might have been if we weren't in church, folks kept talking and telling stories even as we walked out.

"Well, that was just lovely," said Miss Martha as she climbed into the front seat next to Mama. "Just what Old Red would have wanted."

The funeral folks placed a sign on the roof of our car and signaled us to follow along after Eddie and the hearse. We drove slowly down the road, each car getting in line, one after another. I wasn't sure how many cars were in that line, but I bet half of Tucker's Ferry was there, plus folks from the neighboring counties.

As we made our way through the winding back road that led to the graveyard, I stared out the window. It seemed every mile was marked by some memory of Old Red. First there was the parking lot where that school bus had pulled in with Old Red hanging off the mirror, then the muddy river where he'd been baptized, and then the spot where he and Miss Martha had their first taste of moonshine. I wondered if she was remembering that too.

Approaching cars pulled to the side of the road, as if we were an ambulance. Their blinkers flashed. Then they waited for each and every car in our long line to pass.

"I bet that doesn't happen in big cities," said Miss Martha, nodding toward the cars.

As we came to the only stoplight in town, the local police were there, blocking traffic so everyone could get through together. I thought I was done crying, but when I saw that officer standing next to his patrol car, eyes downturned, holding his hat against his chest, well, that opened the floodgates one more time.

Then there we were at the grave, where a small white tent had been placed over a deep hole. After some more words and a prayer from Preacher Jenkins, Old Red was lowered into the ground. Each of us was handed a single carnation. As one final farewell, we all passed by and tossed our flower in. I was the last one. I didn't toss in my carnation, though. Instead, I reached into my bag and pulled out a cluster of blue forget-me-nots that I'd tied with a white ribbon. I'd ordered them special from the flower shop. The petals were wilted and squished, but I knew Old Red wouldn't mind.

When I gazed down, I couldn't help but smile. Old Red had scripted the ceremony from start to finish, but he'd forgotten about one thing—the flowers. And Old Red hated carnations.

May

Pain changes people.

I'm not talking about physical pain, like the kind Tommy had when he fell off our roof and broke his leg. I'm talking about the kind of pain that lives inside a soul. The kind that comes when someone or something folks really care about is suddenly gone. Gone forever.

That kind of pain lingers.

When spring came and I was finally ready to talk about it, I asked Miss Martha how long her pain lasted after she lost her husband.

"It's been fifteen years, Delia," she said. She closed her eyes and smiled as if she was picturing his face. "And it still hurts every day." She had a bundle of wet laundry, and we hung kitchen towels from the line with wooden clips so they could dry. The sun was shining, the air filled with the honeyed scent of new flowers and mountain-fresh detergent.

"Now, mind you, I'm happy, but it took me years to get there."

We moved on to sheets. Each of us grabbing two corners, we snapped out the wrinkles and then stretched the cotton so it would dry flat.

Miss Martha kept talking as we worked. "Grief isn't something you can rush, Delia. When my Wilfred died, it felt like I'd been hit by a flood. One of those flash ones that come up by surprise. That water rushed over, pounding and pushing and holding me down until my lungs screamed. Then my face found the surface and I was able to breathe. When that flood receded, the grief became a tide. It came, it went, it came, it went, and on and on, until finally it was gone most of the time."

I nodded and then hugged Miss Martha tight. There were words in my throat, but I stayed silent. I had a feeling that the tide would come rising up again if I spoke. Not for Miss Martha but for me.

In the shade of her willow tree, the thin, wispy branches all but hiding me, I felt safe. It was like getting hugged without being touched at all. I came to the willow a lot after Old Red died, to think, to write, and to remember.

"Pain heals better when there's noise." That's what Preacher Jenkins told me. I'd gone to talk to him one day, hoping he could lay a hand on my head and heal me like in the Bible stories. He told me he wasn't exactly qualified for that.

"What kind of noise?" I asked.

"The talking kind," he said. Then he reached for a small piece of pottery from his shelf. It had that misshapen, *I did the best I could* look to it. Sort of like the vase I'd made in my fifth-grade art class, the one that tilted to the left like it was taking a rest after hours of standing at attention.

"Look at this cup, Delia. You can see exactly where I've broken it over the years." He pointed to the jagged bits. Each one had been filled in with a different color, so that now, criss-crossing the stone, were streaks of silver and gold. As if lightning had been caught when it struck.

"Why did you color the cracks?" I asked. "Most folks would have tried to make it match so you couldn't see it's broken."

The preacher ran a finger down each seam. "Why try to hide it, Delia? The cracks are what get people talking. And to me, they make it even more beautiful." He laid a hand on my arm. "We've all been broken and healed in different ways."

I've thought a lot about those words. And I've come to realize that in a way this story is my cup. The preacher was right. I do need folks to see the cracks. I need them to ask questions about Old Red and about how it feels when someone you love forgets you, even when those questions are hard to answer. I need to tell the stories about the flowers and the garden and Rosalea, even when the stories make me cry.

When I'm silent, I can feel the cracks getting bigger, stretching wide and going deep. But when I talk, when there's noise and sharing and laughter, something different happens. Bit by bit, I can feel those cracks filling up.

I closed my journal and lay back against the willow. The tide that Miss Martha told me about was coming in. I blinked, taking deep breaths to hold off the tears.

Instead of crying, I decided to visit Old Red. Talking to him always made me feel better. It wasn't a long trip, about the same distance as Riverdale, just in the opposite direction. After parking my bike under a tree I walked, filling my lungs with sunshine and the smell of freshly mown grass and warm dandelions. The clouds shape-shifted in the wind.

For some reason I counted steps, my journal clutched in one hand. From the tree where I left my bike, it took me two hundred sixty-four steps to get to Old Red. He was away from the road, tucked in the middle of a green, grassy field, a tall elm not far away. Against the sky, the leaves reminded me of lace, wispy and delicate.

Rosalea was there too. The stone they shared had been carved for them both after she died. Even Old Red's name and birth date had been carved, the beginning taken care of, so all they needed to finish was the end. My fingers fit perfectly in the groove of the letters.

On my knees, I checked the flowers, pulling off a few withered blossoms and yanking out anything that didn't belong. I had come back in early spring, as soon as the last frost had passed, and planted seedlings. It wasn't exactly like his garden at home, but it was close.

Old Red had always kept Rosalea's grave beautiful. He'd brought me here before, on remembrance days just like this one. Graves in Tucker's Ferry are a sight to behold on remembrance day. There isn't a single one that isn't decorated. Even the really old ones always have a tiny flag or a ribbon.

"Say hi to Rosalea," he'd said when we visited. The first time all I could manage was an awkward hello. Having never talked to a dead person, I wasn't really sure what I was supposed to say.

Old Red didn't have the same concern. He kept up a constant chatter as he weeded and clipped and trimmed, telling her and all those flowers about recent happenings in Tucker's Ferry, the weather, and how much he still loved her.

I'd seen Miss Martha talking to her husband's grave before. But I'd never heard exactly what she said. With Old Red, it was no different than if Rosalea had been there in person. Which she was, I guess.

The cemetery was busy—there were families laying wreaths and tucking blooms into fixed metal vases off in the distance. Closer by, birds called to one another. I could hear the thrum of cars on the highway, and the whisper of the wind through the leaves of that elm. It wasn't quiet, but it was peaceful.

"Hi, Mr. Clancy," I said. "It's Delia."

I sat down, my arms wrapped around my knees.

"Oh, you'd love to be in the garden today. The sun is shining, the sky is filled with cotton-ball clouds, and the earthworms are already digging like mad, tilling up the soil. It's going to be a good year for flowers."

Off in the distance I watched a little girl twirl, her dress floating out around her.

"And guess what? You're never going to believe this." I grinned, just thinking about it. "The new people who bought your house, the Honakers, are sweet as pie. I've been over there a lot. Mrs. Honaker had never seen some of the flowers in your garden, so I've been teaching her the names. *In Latin.*"

Saying that aloud made me laugh. Somewhere, maybe way above me, I could feel Old Red laughing too. Even the flowers at the grave seemed to grin.

"Tommy says hello." I ran my hand over the grass.

We were quiet then for a while. I gazed out over the spring tulips that were now giving way so the other flowers could shine. Tulips always reminded me of those watercolor paint sets I had as a kid, bright spots of primary colors lined up one after the other. Most folks have only the basic red and yellow, but tulips come in more than one hundred different shades. Old Red taught me that.

As I moved my leg it touched the corner of my journal, reminding me it was there. I reached over and picked it up. Then I sat down at the end of the grave and turned to the marked page.

"I've been keeping track of everything that's been happening since my last visit," I said. "Even in heaven you're going to need some new stories eventually."

I told Old Red everything. About how I kept thinking he was going to be sitting on the porch when I passed by, and how Mama let me call Eddie, just to hear Rex growl. I told him that Miss Martha had decided to bake pie every Thursday, because eating it only on holidays just wasn't enough.

"She's gone crazy with the pies!" I laughed and lay back, the flowers touching my face.

Then I gave an update on Mama and Mr. Pete and how they kissed on the porch last week when they thought I was already asleep. And how Miss Carmine was shaving a poodle when it suddenly let out an unexpected sneeze and her shaver went a little wild. I even described how Mae had called me on the phone after she saw that poor dog, and I could barely understand a word she said through all the laughing.

"And Tommy got a sunburn from mowing without a shirt." Thinking about that made me grin. "Mrs. Parker told him it served him right for trying to impress me."

Lying there on that grave, I bet I told Old Red about everyone in Tucker's Ferry. For a small town, there was a lot to talk about. Flipping through the pages of my book, I double-checked to make sure I'd remembered it all.

I'm not sure what I expected when I finished, but a warm, buttery feeling came over me. If Old Red had been there, he'd have asked me to tell all the stories again, not just for him, but for the flowers.

And so I did.

Acknowledgments

The book would not be the same without the influence of some wonderful people.

First, thank you, Dad. You have told me stories since the day I was born, and I still love hearing them. Your tales helped inspire Old Red's.

There is a scene where Tucker's Ferry paints fire hydrants for the Fourth of July. Thanks to my friend Sarah Fedirka and the town of Findlay, Ohio, for that. It fit perfectly.

My writing group, Ellen Ramsey, Jane Resides, and Linda Brewster Rodgers, read and critiqued this book first. You are a special group of women, and I am blessed to have you in my life. Your advice and encouragement is appreciated more than you know.

Thank you to my family, Andreas, Ryan, and Alex. You never complained when I needed to close myself off and write. My best memories include the three of you.

Thank you to my editor, Stephen Roxburgh, whose guidance is always right—even when I ignore it the first (and the second) time. I am so grateful to have you as a mentor and a friend.

And a special thank you to Carolyn Coman. Thank you for listening as I storyboarded this on a hot summer day, for asking the right questions, and for believing in the novel's heart from the very beginning.

Made in the USA
Charleston, SC
20 February 2014